"I CAN'T D̲O̲ ̲..." before she lost her nerve.

Jesse's eyes darkened as they searched her face. He looked more than angry: he looked dangerous. "It feels like you could to me."

"I want to be friends . . . "

"Oh God, not that line!" He released her and fell back against the car in mock defeat.

She took a steadying breath. "You have a job that could take you halfway around the world to-morrow. I'm a homebody. You're a—"

He laced his fingers through hers and singed her with a piercing gaze. "You don't know what I am. What I want."

She felt her resolve falter at the warmth of his fingers entwined with hers. "But I know myself, Jesse. There are things I want one day. I've made some tough decisions lately. Like not dating just for the sake of dating."

"I'm not sure I can be just friends, Lauren. Are you?"

She nodded, hoping she looked more convinc-ing than she felt.

"Okay then." He cupped the side of her face for a moment before he walked to his Jeep.

Lauren watched him go. Her hands, her entire body, were shaking. She could deny it all she wanted, but her body had betrayed her. Betrayed her with the truth. There had never been anyone like Jesse McCain. And she knew there never would be again.

WHAT ARE *LOVESWEPT* ROMANCES?

They are stories of true romance and touching emotion. We believe those two very important ingredients are constants in our highly sensual and very believable stories in the LOVE-SWEPT line. Our goal is to give you, the reader, stories of consistently high quality that may sometimes make you laugh, sometimes make you cry, but are always fresh and creative and contain many delightful surprises within their pages.

Most romance fans read an enormous number of books. Those they truly love, they keep. Others may be traded with friends and soon forgotten. We hope that each LOVESWEPT romance will be a treasure—a "keeper." We will always try to publish

LOVE STORIES YOU'LL NEVER FORGET
BY AUTHORS YOU'LL ALWAYS REMEMBER

The Editors

UP FOR GRABS

KRISTEN
ROBINETTE

BANTAM BOOKS
NEW YORK · TORONTO · LONDON · SYDNEY · AUCKLAND

UP FOR GRABS

A Bantam Book / January 1997

ISBN 0-553-44571-5

Published simultaneously in the United States and Canada

*Bantam Books are published by Bantam Books, a division of Bantam Dou-
bleday Dell Publishing Group, Inc. Its trademark, consisting of the words
"Bantam Books" and the portrayal of a rooster, is Registered in U.S.
Patent and Trademark Office and in other countries. Marca Registrada.
Bantam Books, 1540 Broadway, New York, New York 10036.*

PRINTED IN THE UNITED STATES OF AMERICA

OPM   10 9 8 7 6 5 4 3 2 1

To my husband, Clay,
who buys printers in the rain,
and to my daughters Morgan and Natalie,
who make every day special

Special thanks to Paula,
Shirley, Lucy, and all the ladies
of Heart of Dixie

ONE

"Hush, Lucky!" Lauren Adams said as she tugged the dirt-streaked handkerchief from around her mouth and nose. The weak breeze that played across her face was a rare luxury in the smothering heat, and she allowed herself a few deep breaths of fresh air.

Lauren had more to do that day than she could possibly accomplish, and the puppy's incessant yapping and growling wasn't helping matters. She replaced her makeshift mask and continued to shovel the crumbling hay from the stall, piling it into a weathered wheelbarrow and sending a tornado of dust through the interior of the barn.

Lucky gave another serious growl and jumped against her leg with enough force to knock over a fence post.

"Okay, I'm coming." Lauren straightened and looked around her. The stall, still mounded with dry-rotted hay and years of dust, reflected little of her back-breaking effort. "Well, Rome wasn't built in a day," she muttered as she stuffed her gloves into the back pocket of her shorts and followed the puppy outside.

Shielding her eyes from the midday sun, she scanned the familiar landscape. The farm was isolated in the valley, and the few people who visited were always expected.

Until today. Lauren's breath caught in her throat as she spotted a stranger approaching.

The man was bare-chested, his skin deeply tanned. His tattered blue jean cutoffs had seen better days. Despite his clothes, though, he was no kid. His body had the mature, muscular build of someone in his thirties.

The man called to Lucky in a low, gentle tone. When the puppy began to wag his tail, Lauren's stomach dropped.

"No . . . don't make friends." Lauren glanced around her. She was alone and at least a hundred yards from the house . . . and the phone.

To her relief, the man stopped to kneel at her irrigation pond. He leaned over the reservoir, resting his flat stomach against the rough concrete side that pooled the ice-cold stream water, and splashed his face.

There was undeniable strength in the sinewy shoulders and arms as he pushed himself upright. Lauren watched in frozen fascination as he shook the water from his hair and ran his hands over his damp face. The anxious knot that had settled in the pit of her stomach tightened as he pulled his black hair back into a short ponytail.

A drifter.

In three strides Lauren was back in the barn. She grabbed a rusted pitchfork and tested its weight. It was the only protection she had, so it would have to do. Her chest constricted as she took a steadying breath.

This time as she passed through the barn door, she hesitated in the shadow of the eaves.

The man was blotting his face with a red bandanna, apparently in no hurry to leave. As if he felt her gaze on him, he lowered the material and turned to stare in her direction. Water stood in glistening beads across his wide shoulders and ran in miniature cascades toward the waistband of his faded denim shorts. Instead of acknowledging her presence, he coiled the bandanna into a headband and secured it with a knot at the back of his head.

He walked toward her. Lauren gripped the pitchfork until her fingers ached. She tried to keep the expression on her face casual, but it was almost impossible with her heart drumming like hoofbeats against her chest. To her relief, the man stopped a few feet away. Lucky jumped up, placing his front paws against the stranger's hip. Lauren started to call the puppy back, but hesitated when the man began to rub the dog's head with long, lazy strokes.

The summer breeze carried with it the musky scent of the stranger's sun-warmed skin and the lingering fragrance of soap, sending a sharp pang of awareness through her. Lauren looked into his face and was met with a one-sided, almost amused grin. Had she been staring at him? Suddenly the thin cotton T-shirt she wore seemed unable to protect her from the scorching June sun. When had the day become so unbearably hot?

Her face became hotter as his gaze moved confidently from her eyes to her T-shirt, hesitated, then followed the outline of her shorts and down the length of her legs.

The last of her frayed nerves uncoiled. "This is private property," she blurted out.

A visible shadow settled in the man's eyes, and Lauren was struck by the firm lines of his jaw and high cheekbones. He reached into his back pocket, retrieved a rumpled undershirt, and finished blotting the dampness from his face and neck, apparently totally unconcerned with her statement.

Lauren shifted the pitchfork to her right hand, and watched his gaze follow the tool.

He reached into his other back pocket never looking away from the pitchfork. This time he produced a wrinkled envelope. When he extended it toward her, she almost reached out. "Read it to me," she said instead.

The man looked irritated and heaved a heavy sigh.

His amber-brown eyes glowed like a tiger's against his dark skin. The scowl that lowered his brows only intensified the look, warning Lauren to stay on guard.

"If you have a problem with my being here," he said, "you need to take it up with Mr. Harbison." His voice was deep and gravelly, unlike when he'd spoken to her dog.

"Wh-what?" Lauren stammered.

He shoved the envelope toward her again. "Like it says in the letter, any objections to the excavation were to be put in writing."

"Excavation?" This time Lauren snatched the envelope from his hand. "I don't know what you're talking about."

He slipped the sleeveless undershirt over his head and tugged it into place. "You had ten days from the day you were notified."

The man stuffed the shirttail into his cutoffs, then looked away, allowing her a small measure of privacy while she opened the letter. Lauren noticed his jaw working, sending a play of ripples down his neck and across the exposed, flat muscles of his upper chest.

She turned her attention to the wrinkled paper, and felt the blood drain from her face as she read. The highway department . . . archaeologists from the University of Alabama . . . excavation pending the construction of a possible freeway interchange . . . The words swam before her eyes.

A freeway interchange in Macon Valley? There had to be some mistake. She felt a warm hand grasp the underside of her elbow.

Her grandparents' land. No, her land now. Oh God . . . She had invested every dime she had in renovating the farm into a horse stable.

Lauren looked down at the hand that held her arm, abstractly thinking how tanned the man's skin looked against her own fair skin.

"Hey, are you okay?" The words echoed until they reached the part of her brain that was still functioning.

She jerked her arm free, embarrassed. Then she felt anger welling up and knew there was no stopping it. She didn't want to anyway. Every frustration, every thwarted plan she had made over the last few years took on a new dimension: The promotions given to mediocre male coworkers because they were one of the "good ol' boys," the reassurances that opportunities were on the way if only she would be patient, and then, of course, Roger.

"No, I'm not okay." Of course she wasn't. The good ol' boys still had the upper hand and always would.

"Why don't you sit down for a minute?" The man gestured toward an old lawn chair that she kept next to the barn door. "I assume you didn't know I was coming."

He tried to take her arm again, but she stuffed the envelope into his hand. "I think it's safe to say that." A tear trailed down her cheek, and she numbly wiped it away before meeting his eyes. She squared her shoulders. "I want you off my land."

"Wait a minute." He took a step toward her. "Let me explain."

She placed her hands on her hips. "What could you possibly say?"

He stopped and softened his voice. "That I'll make sure the excavation doesn't disrupt your life, and the damage to your land will be next to nothing." He unfolded the crumpled letter and headed toward the chair without waiting for her. "There's a small-scale map attached to the letter. If you can read an aerial layout, I'll show you where I plan to excavate."

Lauren's body stiffened as she followed him to the chair. "I'm an engineer. At least I was until a couple of months ago." She waved her hand, wanting to erase what she'd unintentionally said. "Anyway, I think I can manage to read your little map."

She was met with another sideways grin. "Sorry," he said, squatting down next to the chair. "Have a seat, then, and I'll explain the notations on my little map."

Lauren felt a small sense of victory as she sat down in the rickety old chair. She scowled at Lucky, however, when the traitorous pup plopped down beside the man.

Ignoring the map, she kneaded her forehead with the

tips of her fingers, trying in vain to rub away the dull ache that had settled there. "What I don't understand, Mr.—" She broke off and met his eyes. "I don't know your name."

"Jesse McCain," he answered, and pulled out his wallet.

"What I don't understand, Mr. McCain—"

"Call me Jesse."

She ignored the offer. "I don't understand where you fit into all of this. Do you work for the state?"

"No, I'm an archaeologist with the university. We're contracted from time to time by the highway department for their big projects." He replaced his wallet in the hip pocket of his shorts. "Our job is to make sure that the land has no historical value before they begin construction."

Before they begin the destruction, she thought. Her hand felt heavy as she smoothed her hair from her damp forehead.

He stood, stretched his legs, and leaned against the outside of the barn. "Listen, don't worry. I'll be out of your way in no time."

His attempt to reassure her only annoyed her. Did he think she was too stupid to see the big picture? His excavation wasn't what upset her; it was the reason for it that sent cold chills down her spine. But she certainly wasn't going to roll out the red carpet for Jesse McCain either.

"The system" was in action again, and her dreams were about to be steamrolled. *Literally.*

"Are you saying the interchange couldn't be built if something valuable was found?" she asked.

"It's possible, but it would have to be a find that really shook up the powers-that-be before it would halt a project." He met her eyes for a moment before looking away. "Anyway, that's not my decision. I just report my findings."

Here we go again, Lauren thought. Was there a man on the face of the earth willing to own up to his own actions? They always seemed to blame it on the other guy. Was that some secret oath males took at puberty?

There was no sense getting into an argument with him, though. It was obvious he lacked the authority to help her.

"Here," he said, "take this in case you have any questions."

She looked up to find him offering her a business card. When she tried to take it from him, he refused to let go until she met his eyes.

"Now you know my name," he said. "But I'm willing to bet you're not Thomas Adams."

Lauren's gaze darted to his mouth, and she noticed for the first time the sensual cast to his lips and the straight white teeth that made his smile so appealing.

"I'm Lauren Adams. Thomas Adams was my grandfather." She averted her eyes from his face. "He died recently and left me this place, which explains the name on your letter and why you startled me."

"I frightened you?"

She nodded. Her gaze unintentionally returned to him, fixing on the thin, damp undershirt that clung to his chest.

He noticed her look and raised his hands in a gesture of apology. "I didn't realize—"

"It's okay."

"No, it's not." He pulled the bandanna from his head. "I should apologize. I came out a couple of weeks ago to introduce myself, but your place was vacant. Today I needed to walk the area, get a feel for the lay of the land. I really didn't expect anyone to be here."

"I've been in the process of moving from my apartment in Birmingham. That also explains the letter. It was probably forwarded to me there." She stood. "You should know that I plan on contacting Mr. Harbison immediately to contest the excavation."

"I really don't think there's any point . . ."

Lauren felt her face redden with anger. "Oh, but there is a point, Mr. McCain." Did he think she would let it go without a fight because he didn't think there was a point? "I've invested everything I have in this place, and I don't intend to stand by while some self-righteous politician plays God with my future."

"But the excavation doesn't necessarily mean—"

"Whether you and the boys down at the highway department are willing to admit your part in this or not, you're involved right up to your nose."

"Don't deny me access, Miss Adams. It'll only make things more difficult for you."

Lauren placed her hands on her hips and raised herself to her full height, which meant the top of her head barely reached his chin. "My grandfather left me a lot of things, Mr. McCain, including a gun cabinet full of rifles."

She walked to the barn door and paused, looking over her shoulder at him. Her body trembled as she worked to control her anger. "And if I see you again, I'll be sure and introduce you to my favorite."

She braced herself for an angry rebuttal, but Jesse McCain only turned and walked away. For a moment Lauren had the crazy urge to call him back. Instead she watched in silence as he made his way across the sun-scorched pasture and into the thicket of woods, disappearing as quickly as he'd arrived.

Lauren sat at her kitchen table surrounded by scribbled notes, empty pistachio hulls, and a now-diluted glass of iced tea. She rested her head against the telephone directory, which was opened to the blue government section.

"I threatened to shoot him." She laughed out loud in the silence of the big old kitchen. "Now I know I've lost my mind."

She raised her head to look at the clock. It was three-thirty. Four hours of senseless telephone calls. She picked up a spiral notebook covered with hastily written information. She had given up on making notes in the margin of the telephone directory when she'd been transferred to the "person in charge" for the third time.

When she had finally been connected with Mr. Harbison's assistant, her worst fears had been confirmed. Her land was one of two sites optioned for the new freeway interchange that would complete the beltway, designed to skirt the city of Birmingham. A press conference would be held to address public concerns, but it wasn't scheduled for months. In other words, she would be informed after the final decision had been made. And of course she had been told not to be too concerned until she heard something definite.

Not to be too concerned!

Lauren thumped the blunt end of her pen against the figures scrawled across the stiff back of the notebook. If she didn't have at least five stalls leased by the end of August, she would have to dip into her savings. And that would only last about a month, before . . . Before what? Before she asked for her old job back at the engineering firm?

She scraped the pistachio hulls onto the notebook, covering the figures, and tossed the shells into the trash with more effort than was necessary. She had tried to continue working at the firm after she'd learned Roger was still married. Tried and failed. Maybe she could have handled it if he'd been just a coworker, instead of her boss. Now she could just imagine what form of gratitude he would expect in return for her old position.

There had to be something she could do. But any way she looked at it, her only hope was Jesse McCain.

Her stomach gave a painful twist. Too many pistachios? No, the truth was, she ached for the chance to rewrite the drama that had taken place between her and Jesse. She was embarrassed by her display of raw emotions. If she had it to do over again, she would be composed, gracious, maybe even allow herself to appear a little vulnerable. That, at least, was a female emotion to which men responded positively.

Instead, she had threatened him with a gun. She looked down at her once-white T-shirt, now covered with smudges of dirt, and winced. Her shorts were even worse. Lucky had left enormous paw prints on the white denim that would probably prove to be permanent.

She kicked out of the soiled boyish clothes and tossed them into the kitchen's laundry alcove. Her ap-

pearance must have been as unappealing to Jesse Mc-
Cain as her behavior.

She made her way up the oak-planked stairs to the
second floor. She was thankful her grandfather had
added a modern showerhead to the old-fashioned bathroom, and turned the faucet to an inviting tepid setting.

She removed her lacy underthings and kicked them
into a corner. The one feminine luxury she had refused
to give up since moving to the farm was pretty lingerie,
although she had happily traded in her tailored suits and
high heels for blue jeans and work boots.

The quick shower was just what she needed to revi-
talize her. Along with the grime, she managed to wash
away much of the anxiety that had built up since she'd
first encountered Jesse. By the time she was towel-drying
her hair, she had formed a plan.

Yes, she had given Jesse McCain every reason not to
like her, which meant he had no incentive to do a thorough excavation. In fact, he could probably juggle a few
rocks and float around in her pond in the name of research without feeling any guilt. She had seen to that.

What she needed was someone on her side, someone
willing to pull out all the stops to help her.

Lauren wrapped up in a terry-cloth robe and padded
back down the stairs, feeling the first stirring of hope.

Opening the bifold doors that hid the washer and
dryer, she found her dirty shorts. She reached into the
front pocket and pulled out the business card with Jesse
McCain's telephone number on it.

She may have gotten off on the wrong foot with the
man, but that was about to change.

Her future just might depend on it.

◆————————◆

"An archaeologist? You mean like King Tut and stuff?"

Normally Jesse would have a snappy comeback designed to make the buxom brunette feel she had just asked the most intelligent question in the world, but this evening he wasn't up to it. He nodded. "Yeah, like King Tut and stuff."

He turned to his friend before the woman could come up with some pointless response. "Listen, Ken, I think I'm going to push off."

Ken Lowell, a fellow archaeologist at the university and reliable drinking buddy, looked at him as though he had lost his mind. And why not? The brunette had arranged her long legs beneath the table so that Jesse couldn't ignore the invitation of her thigh brushing against his. And her friend had draped herself across Ken within minutes of introducing herself. Doubtless, the women were willing to keep them company until closing time, and probably beyond.

"What's eating you?" Ken asked, his wiry dark eyebrows puckering into a straight line.

Jesse stood to stretch his tight muscles. "Nothing, really. Just a full day ahead of me tomorrow."

Ken looked amused. "Aren't you working the Adams site?"

Jesse knew what was coming next. "Yeah, so?"

"Well, poor you!" Ken laughed, squeezing the bare shoulder of the girl nestled against his side. "I should be so lucky."

"For your information, I plan on doing a full excavation."

"What for?" Ken asked, obviously surprised. "The state's not even considering that route."

Jesse swallowed the last of his beer, trying to wash down the guilt that had been gnawing at him all day. He had wanted to tell Lauren Adams the truth, that the other site had secretly been chosen for the freeway interchange. His excavation of her land was merely red tape, a federal requirement that had more to do with convincing the media that both sites had been fairly considered than with anything else.

Telling her, though, would be a recipe for disaster. Jesse had had his fill of disastrous career moves lately. Trust a woman who was being manhandled by the government not to tell her friends and neighbors the truth? Not likely.

The last time he'd gone out on a limb he had almost lost his job. Worse, he'd almost taken the one person he respected with him. From now on he would do his job right down to the last bureaucratic letter, and if that meant covering a few powerful rears, so be it.

Jesse set the beer bottle on the table with a dull thud. If he spent the rest of his career trying to make up for his last lapse in judgment, for what he'd put Professor Ebsin through, it wouldn't be enough.

Still, it had taken all his resolve not to reach out and wipe that damned tear from Lauren Adams's face. His hand jerked in response at the memory, and he shoved it into the pocket of his black jeans, searching for his car keys.

When Jesse didn't answer him, Ken shrugged. "So stay and hang out awhile."

"No thanks. I need to be at the site first thing in the morning."

"Think Big Brother is watching?"

Jesse cocked one eyebrow. "If the university were watching only me, I'd tell them to—"

"You're still worried about Luke?"

"Luke Ebsin doesn't deserve their scrutiny." All the university saw when they looked at the aging professor was an old man, instead of the genius Jesse knew him to be. And that was thanks to him. "I'll be damned if I'll give them another excuse to—"

"That's water under the bridge, Jess," Ken interrupted.

Jesse hesitated. "Let's just say I've seen the winds of change blow often enough when it comes to these things. If the highway department does decide to consider the alternate route, I'll have done my job."

Ken smiled. "True enough."

"Besides, I'm curious about the Adams site." Jesse didn't mention that he was curious about Lauren Adams as well. "The property has three springs, so at the very least I should find Native American occupation."

Ken nodded. "Suit yourself, but it was ninety-eight degrees today. Where do you think I'd be in your shoes?"

"Your shoes would be in the closet, and you'd be napping." Jesse cleared his throat and gave Ken a mocking, stern look. "Unlike what some of my coworkers would do, I don't plan on using this as a vacation."

As Ken grinned, Jesse noticed that the woman sitting next to Ken had slid her hand into the opening of his shirt and was twirling a twist of his thick chest hair between her thumb and forefinger.

For some reason he found the bar atmosphere unappealing that night. Maybe because Lauren Adams probably wasn't enjoying herself right then. She was likely at home, likely distraught, and very likely hating him.

"Sure you don't want to stay?" the brunette at Jesse's side asked in a nasal voice. "Happy hour just started." She shifted in her seat to give him a better view of her deep cleavage, which was spilling out of her tank top.

Jesse indulged himself for a moment. She smiled a pretty, painted pout, no doubt designed to change his mind.

The image of Lauren Adams flashed into his head, her naturally pink lips pulled into a tight, angry line. Her lips should be soft and supple, instead. He wondered what it would take to erase the fear that had made her pretty mouth so defiant. He pictured himself kissing her, sucking gently on her lower lip until it slipped into his mouth.

The beginning of an arousal snapped him back to the present, and an odd mix of surprise and guilt stabbed his gut. Lauren Adams didn't need his kisses, she needed to know the truth. Something he wasn't at liberty to divulge.

"So what'll it be?" Ken asked.

"Huh?" To his embarrassment, Jesse realized he was still staring at, although not really seeing, the brunette's cleavage. But his aroused state had nothing to do with her well-endowed chest and everything to do with the petite blonde who had ordered him from her property. The realization gave him a strange new sense of longing that he couldn't entirely attribute to lust.

He mumbled an excuse and clasped Ken's shoulder in a private appeal for understanding, then he slipped around the table and headed for the exit, guided by the green neon shamrock that glowed above it.

The cooler evening air was a welcome reprieve from the smoky bar, and Jesse leaned his head back as he walked. The smell of freshly cut grass lingered, and the crickets were getting a head start on the darkness, already beginning their faithful song of the night.

Summer reminded him of being a kid. His childhood was definitely something he didn't want to repeat, but summer nights in the South made him feel as close to home as he'd ever come. And considering the number of times his father had moved them when he was a boy, that was an accomplishment.

He unlocked the door of his midnight-blue Jeep Cherokee and slid behind the wheel. After rolling down the windows as he always did, he decided to use his car phone to check his messages. He punched in the series of numbers and symbols, then leaned back against the worn leather seat.

"Mr. McCain, this is Lauren Adams. . . ." Her voice was thin, barely audible over the static of the phone. "I'd like to discuss some things with you . . ." She sounded nervous. Had she been crying? " . . . at your earliest convenience."

Jesse laid the phone down, surprised to find that his pulse had quickened at the unexpected sound of her voice. A voice that had been polite. Too polite. He had liked it better when she was angry. At least then she hadn't seemed so vulnerable.

The sun painted the gray horizon with orange streaks, hinting that only a couple of hours of daylight were left. The digital clock on the dashboard told him it was just six-fifteen. Her place was less than thirty minutes away.

Jesse cranked the Jeep. He knew he'd probably regret it. Being around her any more than necessary would only tempt him to tell her the truth.

More accurately, being around her would simply tempt him. Period.

TWO

Lauren wiggled her toes in her sandals. She would probably be washing bits of grass off her feet in a few minutes, but the sprinklers needed to be turned on. The sun
had finally dipped low enough so that its heat wouldn't
evaporate the precious moisture, and she needed to
make good use of the opportunity.

It was foolish to shower before everything outdoors
had been taken care of, but the distraction had likely
saved her sanity. After drying her hair, she had slipped
on a one-piece cotton sleeper that looked more like a
sleeveless shorts romper than pajamas. She smiled to
herself. Technically she was walking around in broad
daylight in her pajamas, but no one was around to point
it out to her.

She knelt down next to the barn and twisted the
knob that turned on the sprinklers. The pipes groaned
and the water pump gave a curious moan before the
sprinklers began working. Lauren frowned. The noise
sounded as if the pump was struggling, and a broken
water pump was the last thing she needed.

Within seconds, the new blades of grass caught the water and glistened in the early-evening glow.

Lauren was proud of her accomplishments. She had started reworking the small holding pen first, trying to gain some confidence before she tackled the larger pasture. It had taken some time before she'd gotten familiar with the gears of the old tractor, but she'd managed to till and landscape the weed-infested paddock and spread out grass seed.

Now with a little moisture and a lot of luck, the grass would be established by fall . . . just in time for the state's highway decision.

Like catching the edge of an embedded splinter, the seriousness of her situation caused a shudder of fresh pain that killed her sense of achievement. She ran her hands up and down her arms, trying to rub away the chill bumps that had risen despite the heat still trapped in the valley.

Keep busy. That was all she could do until she heard from Jesse McCain. She wondered what he would think of her change of heart, of her suddenly welcoming his excavation. If he was like most men, he would chalk it up to fluctuating female emotions.

Well, that was fine with her. It fit right in with the new image she planned to present to him—damsel in distress. She still wasn't sure she could pull it off. She'd hoped to leave such nonsense to her former coworkers, but she needed to make sure Jesse McCain did a thorough excavation. And how else could she get back on friendly terms with the man?

Lauren made her way into the barn, feeling weary as she noticed all that needed to be done. Whenever the work threatened to overwhelm her, she imagined the stalls filled with horses, friendly nickering, and the homey smell of grain and hay. It would happen, she vowed for the hundredth time.

She looked down at the delicate cotton romper. She didn't want to get dirty, but she needed to set a few mousetraps before nightfall. She had unwisely left a sack of dog food in the barn, and something besides the puppy had helped itself to a meal.

She pulled a bag from the hardware store off the shelf and retrieved the mousetraps. They were the sticky kind, designed to lure the rodent onto adhesive paper. She refused to think about what she would do with her captive in the morning as she placed one trap in the hallway and another on a stall ledge. It was tempting not to set the third trap, but she mustered her determination and climbed the ladder to the loft.

So far, the loft was the only part of the barn that was complete. She had hired a local retiree turned handyman to reinforce the loft floor and had stocked it with fresh bales of Bermuda hay, taking advantage of the spring cutting. It was swept clean, and the hay gave off such a wonderful sweet smell that the sweltering heat was almost bearable.

She had just unwrapped the trap and placed it in a likely corner when she heard the sound of a car's engine. She cocked her head, listening. Gravel crunched and popped as the unmistakable sound of a car coming down the drive grew louder. Lauren rushed to the open loft door and looked down as a Jeep came to a halt in her driveway.

Lucky, who had launched into a frenzied barking when the Jeep approached, now wagged his tail as the door opened and Jesse McCain stepped out.

"No, no, no!" she heard herself say out loud before she clapped her hand over her mouth.

She quickly examined her romper. Would he know she was wearing something designed for sleeping? She remembered the model's pose in the mail-order catalog. Sleep wasn't the only thing the outfit was designed to encourage.

There was no way she was coming out of hiding until he left, but it had to be well over one hundred degrees in the loft. She smoothed her unbound hair away from her face, surprised to feel moisture beading on her forehead. If she had worn any makeup, it would have already melted into a mess.

She peeked around the loft door again, noticing how different Jesse appeared in regular clothing. He made a striking figure from her vantage point. His white polo shirt made his short ponytail and the black jeans he wore stand out in sharp contrast.

She squatted down and discreetly watched as he strode toward the house, dipping his head to keep from hitting the clematis vine that formed an arch at the porch entrance. He rang the doorbell.

"Go away, go away. . . ." she whispered.

He rang the doorbell a second time and occupied himself by admiring a huge purple clematis blossom.

"Nobody's home," Lauren said in a singsong voice. "Now go away."

He didn't. Instead he turned toward the barn.

The sprinklers. She'd forgotten about them. They were acting like a magnet, drawing him toward her hiding place. She ducked her head back through the door, and was immediately sorry. The ground below and the loft floor reeled and melded into one before her eyes.

She plopped down on her rear and mopped her sweaty forehead with the back of her hand. She shouldn't have squatted in one position for so long. The loft was spinning in earnest now, and she felt queasy. If only it weren't so damned hot, she thought.

"Lauren?" Jesse called, now immediately below her.

In just a minute he'll give up, she reassured herself. Then she would get some air, and the spinning would stop. After everything she'd been through that day, why was this happening?

She heard Lucky scurry to the ladder, which was nothing more than a series of narrow boards nailed to the barn wall, and begin pawing at the wood. He barked, and the shrill noise echoed up the shaft, seeming to penetrate straight into her head.

It was mattering less to Lauren every minute whether Jesse discovered her or not. She only wanted the nausea to pass. The air was so hot and heavy, she felt she would smother to death if she didn't get some fresh air soon.

She rested her head on her knees. Water. She wanted water. A huge glass of ice water.

As if from a long way away, she heard the sound of Jesse's boots on the narrow boards of the ladder. When the noise stopped, she lifted her head from her knees and found his face peeking over the top of the ladder shaft, just inches from her feet.

"I'm not being set up for an ambush, am I?" He was holding the top rung of the ladder and rocking playfully back and forth, intensifying her dizziness.

Lauren noticed that his hair, now dry, wasn't one length after all, but fell in long soft layers about his face.

She wondered how it would look with the short ponytail unbound.

Her hand lifted, then dropped to her side. Had she started to reach for the rubber band that held it? No, she wasn't feeling that light-headed. She would die of embarrassment if she did something so absurd.

A puzzled look crossed his face, and she blinked, suddenly wondering how long she had been staring at him. She needed to pull her disjointed thoughts together, explain why she was sitting in the barn loft in her pajamas.

"Are you okay?" he asked.

She looked over her shoulder, waving in the general direction of the mousetrap in the corner. "I was just setting a mousetrap," she said.

He chuckled. *"That's* a mousetrap?"

"They stick to the paper when they walk on it."

He stared at her again, his brow furrowing in a look of concern. She felt him scrutinizing her face.

"I don't like the thought of . . . you know, a real mousetrap," she heard herself say without intending to say anything more.

"You mean the kind with the little metal bar that goes splat?"

She nodded.

Jesse smiled, his teeth flashing white in the growing shadows of the loft. She met his eyes. They were brown, but the numerous bursts of gold within them made them look amber. He was beautiful, no doubt about it. Lauren closed her eyes.

"Listen, it's hotter than hell up here," he said. "Can we talk somewhere a little cooler?"

She looked at the edge of the floor where it gave way to the shaft, knowing she would have to trust her arms to lower herself over the edge until she had a good foot-hold on the ladder. She bit her lip. Honestly, she didn't think she could.

"I was just sitting here a minute." She gestured toward the high ceiling of the loft, waving her hand as if she were shooing the hot air out the door. "The heat kind of got to me."

"How long have you been up here?"

She stared wordlessly at him. Judging from the suspicious, slightly irritated look on his face, he knew she had been hiding.

"Never mind," he said. "Scoot toward the edge."

Oh great, that's what my gynecologist always says, Lauren thought, and laughed out loud. Jesse cocked one eyebrow in question. "What's so funny?"

"Nothing, really." She inched toward the shaft, wondering if he thought she was crazy.

"Swing your feet over and find a rung. I'll stay where I am in case you get shaky."

She nodded.

"Put one hand on my shoulder and hold the floor with the other."

Their eyes met.

"It's okay. Go ahead," Jesse said.

Lauren swung her legs over and concentrated on finding the top rung with the slick leather bottom of her sandal. Finally her left foot met solidly with the wood. She placed her palm against Jesse's shoulder, and through the thin cotton of his shirt, she felt his muscles tense at the contact.

She looked up into his face, and found that he was smiling. It was the kind of smile she'd grown accustomed to using herself before she'd left her job, a smile designed to maintain appearances while another emotion was seething just below the surface.

Lauren felt suspended, knowing she was about to lower herself into a near stranger's arms. The thought was inviting, and that in itself disturbed her.

She smoothed her hair away from her face as another wave of heat crashed over her, scattering her thoughts. She was thankful he was there. For a moment she imagined how easy it would be to wrap her arms around his neck and let him lower them both to the ground. She had no doubt he could.

She shook her head. The logical thing to do would be to place her other foot on the next rung so that she could rotate her body toward the ladder and descend on her own.

"Cold feet?" Jesse's voice broke the silence, startling her.

"Right now I'd settle for cold *anything*." She smiled weakly before lowering her right foot down the shaft.

The rung was farther down than she had anticipated, and her arms began to tremble. She squeezed her eyes shut, willing herself not to collapse. Finally, her sandal tapped against the wood.

Everything seemed to go perfectly still as the scent of him surrounded her. He was so close. The smell of his skin was warm and undeniably male. When she opened her eyes, she found herself staring at the open V of his shirt.

They were only a breath apart, yet their sole contact was her hand still resting on his shoulder. And, she realized, the underside of her arm as it trailed across his chest. Suddenly aware of it, the heat from that contact raised the delicate hairs on her arm, but she didn't move.

Lifting her gaze a few inches, she focused on the hollow of his neck. She could see his pulse moving the skin in a hypnotic rhythm. It was fast. Steady but very fast. She closed her eyes again. Knowing he couldn't see her, she smiled as she inhaled the spicy scent of soap and the intoxicating aroma that was simply Jesse McCain.

"Oh, to hell with this!" he said suddenly.

Lauren felt his arm against the backs of her knees before she landed against his chest. The fading light from the loft door flashed before her eyes as she tilted to and fro. She shut her eyes, trying to still the dizzy feeling. As she felt the two of them descending, she wadded the soft material of Jesse's shirt in her hand. If she fell, she was taking him with her.

When the rocking sensation became a steady rhythm, she opened her eyes and found herself being carted toward the house.

"You can put me down now," she said, squirming against his grip.

"That's okay."

She looked up at his face, set in determined lines. "I'm serious," she said. "Put me down."

He glanced at her, his features softening somewhat. "Let's get you to the house first."

"I'm okay!" Lauren twisted, freeing herself. Her feet landed with a crunch on the gravel road. She must have swayed, because Jesse's arm snaked out to steady her. His hand gripped her upper arm.

"You're okay, huh?" He looked annoyed again. "From what I saw, you were about to melt into a pretty little puddle up there!"

"Well, I wouldn't have been if you . . ."

"If I what? What did I do?" He released her arm.

"You showed up here unannounced and I . . ." She looked down. "I wasn't dressed."

His gaze followed hers. He was examining her, there was no other way to describe it. He made one quick observation, then began again, this time with excruciating thoroughness.

The rush that filled Jesse was akin to what he felt when he held a priceless artifact in his hands. Only he wasn't holding Lauren Adams. He wanted to, though. Oh, he wanted to. He shifted, hoping to hide the effect she was having on his body. But there was no denying to himself how much he wanted her when he saw her nipples brush against the soft material that covered them.

"You look fine to me." His voice was husky, and he realized the comment sounded like a tired come-on. It was too late; the words had already left his mouth.

She blushed, and for a moment he wondered if she would take offense after all—until she crossed her arms over her breasts, blocking his view. The thought of her breasts pressed against the bare backs of her arms brought a fresh swell of desire.

"What are you doing here?" she asked.

"*You* asked to see *me*, remember?"

"I . . . I left a message on your answering machine. I didn't think you'd get it until you went to work in the morning."

"That was my home number."

She put her hands on her hips. The loose-fitting outfit clung to her waist, and he realized how petite she was.

"What was your home number doing on your business card? Why didn't you use your office number?" She fired the questions at him.

He laughed, despite the uncomfortable ache that had

settled between his legs. "Nine times out of ten, this is my office." He gestured toward the wooded valley. "I spend very little time at the university. Not enough to put the number down."

"Oh." The sound she made was barely a whisper.

"Look, I'm sorry I surprised you. But was it such a big deal that you needed to hide out in the barn until you got sick?"

"I wasn't hiding exactly." She shifted from foot to foot, and he realized she was looking paler by the second. "I was turning on the sprinklers. Listen, speaking of water, I could use a drink."

Jesse followed her as she walked toward the house. She was still woozy, he thought. Otherwise, she would have gotten rid of him by now.

Well, he didn't intend to be so easy to dismiss this time. After all, he needed to make sure she was okay. That was his motivation, wasn't it? Anything else seemed selfish on his part, especially considering the distress he'd caused her.

He expected her to go inside the house, but she knelt by a garden hose at the foot of the porch stairs instead. She let the water run for a moment, then began to drink in huge gulps, her eyes closed as if she were enjoying some private ecstasy.

When she finally stood up, though, he knew by the glassy look in her eyes that she was going to faint.

Jesse barely had time to move behind her before she went limp. The top of her head hit his lower lip as he caught her, and he muttered a soft curse, already tasting blood. Gathering her into his arms, he made his way to the stairs and sat down, positioning her upright on the stair below him and securing her bare shoulders between his knees. He reached for the garden hose and tugged on it until he held the open end.

"Lauren?" he called, stroking the side of her face. Her features remained relaxed.

He carefully aimed the hose so that the cold water rushed over the pulse point of one ankle. She stirred but didn't come to. He held it there a minute, allowing the water to work its cooling magic, then shifted it to the other ankle. He wondered what her response would be when she discovered her waterlogged sandals.

He was surprised that she hadn't roused yet. Surely it was nothing more than the heat. Making a crimp in the hose, he raised her hair and allowed a small trickle to flow across the back of her neck.

"What is . . . Quit it!" She slapped at his hands as she came to.

He threw the hose to the ground and grasped her shoulders. "Lauren, it's okay."

She whirled to face him, still cradled between his knees. "What happened? What were you doing that for?"

Jesse conjured up his most charming smile. "Do you always ask two questions at once?" He knew she would be angry at herself for losing control and that he was about to become the target of that anger.

His smile faded at the sight of her wet clothing. Her breasts had reacted to the cold water, her nipples contracting to sharp peaks and teasing him by not being fully revealed through the floral material. He felt himself falling into a cauldron of desire so intense, it was almost painful.

"What happened?" she repeated.

"You fainted."

Lauren shook her head, cutting her eyes in his direction. "I don't faint. Ever."

"There's a first time for everything. And don't look at me like that. All I did was catch you."

"And hose me down!" She stamped her sandals. "I've never fainted before in my life." A strange expression crossed her face. "Oh . . ."

"What?"

"It's nothing." She pressed her hand to her stomach. "I just remembered why I got so light-headed."

A dozen reasons came to mind, the first of which was that she was pregnant. Jesse's gaze flashed to her abdomen, finding nothing but a slender waist. She had said that she'd moved from her apartment to the farm, but she'd never said she was living here alone.

"The pistachios," she said.

"Huh?"

"All I ate for lunch were pistachios. I was turning the sprinklers on before I fixed myself something else. That's when you came."

Jesse breathed a sigh of relief, suddenly feeling a little guilty. Again. "Listen, I'm sorry about everything."

She wrinkled her nose as she tried to adjust the water-soaked top of her sleeper. "What did you do this for?"

"I was cooling your pulse points to get your body temperature back down."

"Thanks. I think." She looked as if she didn't know whether to continue to hold the fabric away from her body or to let it drop back against her breasts.

"You sounded anxious to talk to me," he said. "What did you want to discuss?"

She glanced away as if she was hiding something. "It

can wait. I realized that I never took a look at the aerial layout, and I had a few other questions." She waved her hand in the air. "But nothing that can't wait until morning."

Well, one point was obvious enough, Jesse thought. She was dismissing him again. He looked about him at the growing darkness. The katydids had joined the crickets, and their chanting was difficult to ignore. A gentle night breeze rustled the leaves of the azaleas that grew like matching sentinels on either side of the stairs. He was sure Lauren was uncomfortable in her wet clothes. But he was even more certain that he wasn't ready to leave.

"What were you about to fix?" he asked.

"What?"

"When I drove up. What were you about to fix yourself to eat?"

"Oh." She looked confused. "Actually I hadn't given it much thought."

Jesse stood and walked to the top of the stairs. He tried the front door. It was unlocked, but instead of opening it, he pushed against it with his hip.

He looked over his shoulder at Lauren, who was scowling at him from the foot of the stairs. "Do you always lock your front door when you go to the barn?" he asked.

"It's not locked. Anyway, what are you doing?"

"I'm telling you it's locked." He shoved against it again for emphasis.

Lauren stood, and as Jesse noted her still pale complexion, he wondered if she was okay. He smiled when she grasped the black wrought iron railing, swaying only slightly, and marched to the top of the stairs, pushing him aside.

"I know I didn't lock . . ." She stumbled through the front door as it swung easily against her weight.

"You must have a special touch." Jesse stifled a grin as he followed her through the entrance. "Now, point me toward the kitchen and I'll fix you something to eat."

She was staring at him, her jaw slack as if she couldn't figure out how he'd managed to weasel his way in without an invitation. "No," she finally said. She gathered her composure. "I mean, I appreciate everything, but I'm sure you have things to do."

"Let me rephrase that then. You run along and change clothes"—he nodded toward her wet romper, another grin tugging at his mouth—"and I'll fix *us* something to eat."

"You haven't eaten?"

"Your message sounded so imperative, I left without eating."

She flipped a light switch on the wall, illuminating an ornate old chandelier, then narrowed her eyes and looked up into his face as if trying to determine if he was lying. As he had hoped, her Southern hospitality won out.

"The kitchen is straight ahead," she said. "Have a seat and I'll be right back to fix us something."

He watched the hem of her romper rise and fall as she climbed the wide staircase.

"I hope you don't mind a sandwich," she called over her shoulder as she reached the top stair.

He met her eyes and found an odd mix of emotions playing across her face. She had caught him staring. Did she know how badly he wanted to follow her up the stairs, to pull her against his body and taste the smooth, damp nape of her neck?

"That sounds delicious," he said.

Lauren managed to keep her expression neutral as she nodded and walked away, but every alarm in her head was going off. She wasn't comfortable with Jesse in her house, even though he'd been nothing but a gentleman.

What was it she had told herself she should do—be a damsel in distress? Well, she couldn't have played the part any better if she'd tried. But instead of feeling rescued, she felt ridiculous. No, she'd leave the damsel in distress ruse to someone else. The role just didn't suit her.

Her hands shook as she rummaged through her bureau drawer, eventually finding a conservative pair of cotton shorts and a summer top. Tugging the straps of her sleeper from her shoulders, she stepped out of the damp garment and kicked off her sandals. She breathed a sigh of relief as she pulled a bra into place.

After dressing, she ran a brush through her hair, applied an almost transparent lipstick, and pulled on a pair of tennis shoes. Now that she was fully dressed, she felt she was on somewhat equal ground. The thought gave her confidence as she hurried back downstairs to the stranger in her kitchen.

As she rounded the corner, the mouthwatering aroma of bacon frying hit her. Her eyes flew wide open.

Jesse stood with his back to her, a pink gingham dish towel tossed over one shoulder and an oven mitt covering his left hand. He held a fork over her grandmother's old iron skillet and was engrossed in his task of flipping the bacon. Something inside her chest ached, and for a moment she clutched at an emptiness inside that she couldn't quite define.

She was almost directly behind him when he heard her. "Hey, that was quick." He nodded toward her change of clothes. "You didn't even give me time to finish."

Lauren felt welded to the floor.

"I'm making BLTs," he went on, ignoring her silence. "I hope you have the lettuce and tomato to go with the bacon."

She nodded, not knowing what to say. He was standing at her stove cooking as if it were the most natural thing in the world.

She hardly knew the man!

She was groping for the right words to make that point without seeming ungrateful, when she noticed his swollen lower lip. He caught her stare and ran his tongue over the small cut. Lauren felt her knees weaken at the gesture.

"Just a battle wound." He threw his head back, dislodging a lock of hair that had fallen across his forehead.

"The battle being me?"

"Yeah, but I won." He winked playfully at her.

She raised her eyebrows. "You don't look like you won."

"Any man who gets to hold a scantily clad woman wins." He waved the oven mitt in the air. "It's been that way since the beginning of time."

Lauren hid her blush by turning her back to him. "Let me get you something for it," she said, opening the kitchen cabinet that held various over-the-counter medicines. She found a crinkled tube of antibacterial ointment and extended it toward him. "This might help."

"Will you do me the honor?" he asked, tilting his head down.

She stared at him, not moving.

He held up his hands, the fork in one and the oven mitt covering the other. The bacon popped, and he glanced behind him. "Better hurry."

She tugged the fork from his grip. "The bathroom is up the stairs and to the right." She replaced the fork with the ointment.

If he felt any disappointment, Jesse's face didn't reveal it. Instead, he smiled and tossed the oven mitt to her before bounding for the stairs, leaving her wondering if she had misread the sensual tone in his voice.

She ripped two paper towels away from the roll and transferred the bacon to them. She was clenching her jaw, a bad habit developed on her old job. Then it hit her. *She* was the one feeling rejected.

Impossible, she told herself. Hadn't she looked forward to escaping such advances when she left her job? He was the one who had conned her into an invitation to supper. If she had any sense, she would put his sandwich into a paper bag—to go!

By the time she heard him return, Lauren had toasted wheat bread and added a small amount of mayonnaise and lettuce to each sandwich. When she looked up, she saw that Jesse had a large map tucked under one arm and was tossing a tomato into the air with his other hand.

"Do you already have one?" he asked, holding the tomato up for her inspection.

"No, I don't. Thank you." Her voice reflected her irritation.

"Don't thank me, I got it off your vine." He offered

her the tomato. "I noticed it when I went out to the Jeep."

She reached for the tomato. When she touched its soft, ripe skin, she hesitated. It was still warm from the sun, yet it was as if she were feeling the heat from Jesse's palm. As the warmth radiated through her, she felt such a genuine wave of desire, her head swam.

She fashioned a casual expression and looked up into his face. His swollen lip was now moist from the ointment. She forced herself to meet his eyes. "I hope you don't mind it with the skin on." She slid the tomato from his hand.

"Peeling the skin off is for sissies," he said. "Are you feeling okay?"

"Yes, just unbelievably hungry."

She poured two glasses of iced tea and sliced the tomato in record time. It seemed as soon as they sat down at the massive oak table in the kitchen, she had finished her sandwich. She felt Jesse's gaze on her and looked up.

"You weren't kidding about being hungry, were you?" His lopsided grin made him look boyish.

Crumbs were scattered beyond the edge of her plate, and in an effort to hide her embarrassment, Lauren herded them into a pile. "No, I wasn't. It's amazing how much better I feel." She noticed that he seemed to be thoroughly enjoying his sandwich as well. "I guess you weren't kidding either." She nodded toward the remainder of his sandwich as it disappeared into his mouth.

"You don't think I would try to dupe you out of a free meal, do you?"

Lauren shrugged as she stood and cleared their plates. She thought it best to change the subject. "My grandmother had an old container filled with Indian arrowheads that the grandkids found over the years. I was wondering if it would help you to go through them."

His expression brightened with undeniable interest. "I'd love to."

Lauren was elated. Seeing the spark that lit his eyes renewed her hope. "I looked around for them this afternoon but couldn't find them. But I know they're here somewhere." She began to pace the floor. "I'll look again right away."

"Hang on. I don't want to get your hopes up. Arrowheads are pretty common in this area. I'm just curious about them."

"Oh, I see." She saw a look of sympathy in his eyes, and the bit of hope she had died. She felt helpless to protect her own home.

"I'll let you know if I come across them then," she said as she stacked their plates in the sink.

Without asking, she unrolled the map on the kitchen table, frowning as she attempted to orientate herself with the topographical layout.

Jesse moved to stand behind her. "The boundaries of your property are highlighted in yellow," he said, tracing a long finger across one line. "Each of the sites I plan to excavate are indicated by a red *X*."

"Hmm, the last site is near the mouth of Turtle Creek. How do you plan to get your equipment in?"

He tapped a thin line near a two-lane highway. "This is an access road I plan to use."

She shook her head. "It was an access road before a tornado hit a couple of years ago. It's not really a road now, there are so many trees down."

"Damn," he muttered. "I didn't walk that area yesterday, but judging from the lay of the land, it looked like it might be the most productive site."

"Really?" She knew she was setting herself up for a major disappointment by clinging to the possibility that he would find something of enough value to halt the project, but it was her only hope so far. "You can still get to it by coming across my property."

"How?" He squinted at the map.

"I'll take down two sections of fence at the barn paddock. There's an old logging road you can follow from there."

"Do you mean the paddock next to the barn?"

She nodded.

A strange expression crossed his face. "It looks like that paddock was just seeded."

"It was." A small laugh escaped her, and she bit her lip, thinking about the backbreaking work she had done to prepare it. "But in the end, it doesn't matter whether it's me or the state that destroys it." She shrugged. "You and the others need to get your trucks and equipment through. That's the bottom line."

She thought she heard him moan. "You don't need to sacrifice your hard work for me, Lauren."

"Not just for you." She knew she was close to tears, and fought for control. "The only way the highway department will back off is if you find something to stop them." She straightened her shoulders. "So I intend to help you."

Silence hung between them for a moment before Jesse snatched up the map, allowing it to swiftly coil back up. He pounded it against his palm as he moved to stare out the kitchen window. "You don't understand."

Lauren stared at his back, puzzled by his reaction to her honesty.

He turned to face her. Leaning against the counter, he spread his arms in a gesture of defeat. "There are no *others*. I'm the only one assigned to the excavation. And what equipment I'll need can be carried by hand."

He was the only one? There was no way one person could tackle a job that size. Then reality hit her like a ton of bricks. Of course. They had already chosen the route. And her home—her dreams—would be destroyed by bulldozers and dynamite.

The excavation was all for show. She squeezed her eyes shut. What had made her think everyone else took this as seriously as she did? After all, it was only her life they were ruining, nothing nearly as important as the next election.

"Lauren?"

Her anger rose from the pit of her stomach, and she felt as if it physically slammed into her head. She could feel the pounding of her pulse behind her eyes as they filled with tears.

"They've already decided on this route, and they'll go ahead with the interchange no matter what you find, won't they?" she asked.

An odd expression crossed his face. "No, it's not like that. . . ."

Hands on her hips, she walked over to stand toe-to-toe with him. "I have a can of red spray paint in the barn. I'll bet you could take it to the nearest rock and write 'Jesse McCain was here' and they would thank you for a job well done. This is all just a ruse to them. Isn't that right?"

He gazed down into her eyes, and she had to look

away from the pity she saw there. "I wish I could explain." His voice faltered.

"You should leave." She pointed toward the back door, her gaze level with his chest.

She felt as if she would shatter into a million pieces if he protested. She didn't have the strength to fight him and the rest of the world too.

When his warm hand brushed her face, she instinctively leaned toward him. But reality snapped her back, and she recoiled from his touch with a defiant jerk. The truth was, no matter what attraction she felt for Jesse McCain, he wasn't on her side.

She was on her own.

He reached for her again, and she knocked his arm away, dislodging the map he had tucked beneath his arm. It fell to the floor with a hollow thud and skidded beneath the kitchen table.

She looked up and met his eyes, the amber bursts within them bright with a light she couldn't define. "Go." She pointed again to the door.

This time he grasped her face with tender force, urging her chin up so she couldn't look away. "I am not the enemy, Lauren." Barely checked emotion turned his voice to a gravelly whisper.

Before she could react, he released her and was through the door, leaving her with only the lingering warmth of his touch.

THREE

Part of Lauren's brain tried to ignore the ringing, while another groped through the haze of sleep so she could answer the phone. Eventually, she pulled the receiver to her ear. "Hello?"

"Hey, you weren't asleep, were you?" Her younger sister's cheerful voice grated in her ear. "I thought all you country folks got up with the chickens."

"Cassie? What time is it?" She sat up, squinting at the digital clock on her dresser. "It's nine-thirty!"

"Okay, what gives? You're never asleep at this time of day, even if it is Saturday." Cassie paused. "Oh wow . . . I'm sorry! Have you got a guy there?"

Inwardly Lauren groaned. Cassie was her opposite when it came to men. While they looked enough alike to be twins, with their straight blond hair and dark blue eyes, more than just the five years' difference in their ages separated them. Their outlooks on life differed drastically, their views on men being only one case in point.

"No, I do not have a guy here." Lauren tugged her

ponytail holder free, allowing her hair to fall across her shoulders. "Since when have you known me to wake up with a guy?"

"Sadly, never." Cassie barely paused before she plunged ahead. "I thought maybe old roving Roger was with you."

"Cassandra Adams, do you never tire of this conversation?"

"Well?" Cassie wasn't the type to be easily discouraged.

"No, I'm afraid there's not enough room in my bed for him, his wife, and his kids."

Cassie grunted. "When are you going to stop beating yourself up over that? He failed to tell *you* that he was married, remember?"

Lauren moaned, still blinking the sleep from her eyes. "Can we skip this, Cassie? I already know how the story ends."

The truth was, men were Cassie's favorite subject, and Roger was the only living, breathing topic Lauren had provided her sister over the last few years. And no matter how many times Lauren tried to convince her otherwise, Cassie continued to act as if he'd broken Lauren's heart. Permanently numbed it maybe, but he hadn't broken it.

"Do you have any plans?" Cassie asked, finally obliging her by changing the subject.

Lauren hesitated, thinking how futile it seemed to continue working on the barn, but she couldn't just sit around and do nothing.

"I need to drain the irrigation pond and take a look at the water pump. It's been making a terrible noise and—"

"Thank God you delivered me from such a fate when you offered to buy out my half of that place!" Cassie interrupted. "I swear it's all you ever think of. What I meant is, what are you doing tonight?"

"You mean you want to do something with me—with Lauren you-bore-me-to-tears Adams?" She feigned difficulty breathing. "I thought you stayed too busy peddling houses to make plans with me."

"Well, I've sucked all the blood from the local wealthy, and I wanted to check out a new restaurant called the Green Shamrock Pub."

It was on the tip of Lauren's tongue to say no, that she had too much work to do, but the truth was she needed to discuss her situation with Cassie. Not just to have someone to talk to, but to prepare her. Her sister might be a little on the flighty side, but she was shrewd when it came to money. And money was what Lauren still owed Cassie for her half of their grandparents' estate.

"Okay."

"Okay?" Cassie sounded sincerely shocked. "What's gotten into my big sister? Sleeping until nine-thirty in the morning and taking me up on a night out!"

"Believe me, I could use a night out. Yesterday was possibly the worst day of my life."

"Men troubles?"

Lauren considered that a moment before she answered. "You could say that."

She could practically hear Cassie smacking her lips in anticipation. "I can hardly wait to hear all about it! I'll pick you up at seven."

Instead of braving the heat, Lauren spent the remainder of the morning at the library, checking out every available volume on Alabama archaeology and Native American artifacts. Back home she curled up with several books on southeastern spear points and pottery, and the afternoon flew by as she read, committing as many facts as she could to memory.

At six-thirty she looked at the antique clock on the kitchen wall, more content to stare at the swinging pendulum than she was to get ready for her evening out with her sister. Maybe she could cancel. The idea had tempted her several times during the past hour. But no. She'd never hear the end of it from Cassie if she did.

Lauren made quick work of showering, and chose a blue short-sleeved silk top and matching silk trousers. The top was fitted at the waist, which flattered her slim figure and highlighted her darker blue eyes. Most importantly, the outfit was cool.

The same train of thought made her pull her hair up, coiling it into a loose twist and fastening it at the crown. She had just finished applying mascara and rose-tinted lipstick when she heard the front door open.

Cassie's voice echoed in the foyer. "Your dream date is here!"

"Hey, dream date, you're early!" Lauren pressed her lips together, smoothing her lipstick. "Come on up."

Cassie entered the bedroom in time to see Lauren sliding on a pair of buckskin-colored flats. "Jeez, you're not wearing those, are you?"

"Why not?"

"Because you're not mucking out a stall, that's why not. Wear some heels, shortie." Cassie was two inches taller than Lauren and never let her forget it.

Lauren looked into her sister's face, which would have been alarmingly identical to her own if it weren't for Cassie's pixielike haircut, and groaned. Rather than argue, she disappeared into her closet and reemerged wearing low-heeled sandals.

With the same energy she used to sell real estate, Cassie rushed Lauren to finish getting ready, pushed her out the door, and had her buckled into the passenger's seat of her red Mustang almost before Lauren could blink. When they screeched to a stop in the parking lot of the Green Shamrock, Lauren sent up a quick prayer of thanks, feeling as if she had just survived a maniacal roller-coaster ride.

It took a moment for her eyes to adjust to the dark as they entered the Green Shamrock. She raised her voice to be heard over the music. "You said it was a restaurant."

"It is! For your information, they are supposed to have very good food here."

Lauren rolled her eyes.

"Well, God forbid it should have a dance floor!" Cassie threw her hands in the air. "You're about to turn thirty, not ninety, Lauren."

Lauren gave her a warning look at the mention of her looming thirtieth birthday. Her sister was right, though. Her isolation at the farm had been like a healing balm, and the stress and bitterness she had felt at her old job had all but disappeared. But maybe she had been away from people for so long, she'd forgotten how to have a good time.

"I didn't say I objected," Lauren said as the hostess ushered them to a table. "But I need to discuss something with you, and I don't know if you can hear me over the noise."

A serious expression erased Cassie's smile. "Is something wrong?"

Lauren didn't try to answer her sister until they were seated. Then, to her surprise, the story poured nonstop from her until every detail was told and she was breathless from the effort.

Cassie stared at her, her eyes round and her red-tipped fingernails drumming out an unnerving cadence on the imitation wood tabletop. "So this Jesse McCain fellow has the hots for you, huh?"

Lauren couldn't believe her ears. "What? Is that all you have to say? I pour out my heart to you and all you can think about is the fact that I met a man!"

"So you admit it then?"

"Admit what?" Lauren could feel the blood rushing to her face and knew that the tip of her nose was red with indignation. "There is nothing to admit. Do you think it was easy to tell you this? All my money is tied up in Grandfather's estate. If I lose it, I may never be able to repay you." She flattened her sister's hand against the table with her own, stopping her drumming. "You could stand to lose a great deal, Sis, so pay attention to what I'm saying."

"I don't care."

"What?"

Cassie pulled her hand away and leaned across the table. "I said, I don't care, and I mean it. Besides, it's no fun spending money I didn't earn."

Lauren brushed away a tendril of hair that had escaped its twist and tried to hide the pain she felt at her sister's comment. Cassie noticed anyway.

"Oh wow, Lauren, I'm sorry." She tugged Lauren's hand across the table, turning it palm upward. She poked a thick callus with the tip of her perfectly manicured fingernail. "This is what I call earning it." Uncharacteristic tears filled Cassie's eyes. "You know, Grandfather and Grandmother would be proud of the way you're fixing up the place. Lord knows Mom and Dad have no intention of taking care of it."

Lauren's first instinct was to scold Cassie on her parents' behalf, but there was a ring of truth to what her sister said. "Retiring to Florida was what they wanted, and they deserve to be happy."

Cassie shrugged. "I just find it sad that they don't have any ties to the land."

Lauren knew what Cassie really meant. It still seemed strange that her parents could distance themselves, at least physically, from her. And ironic that Lauren had followed in her father's footsteps and become an engineer. Ironic because it wasn't until her parents had moved away, until her father was no longer there to applaud her achievements, that Lauren discovered she wasn't really happy.

Of course, Roger had been the straw that broke the camel's back. And now she found it unbelievable that her dreams could be taken away from her just as she'd discovered what they truly were.

Suddenly Cassie's grim expression was replaced with her most charming smile, and Lauren looked up to find a handsome young waiter beaming down at her sister. She shook her head as Cassie engaged him in a serious conversation about what ingredients went into the restaurant's specialty drink. After a few minutes he trotted off to fill her order, promising to return as quickly as possible.

True to his word, they were each sipping an icy pink

concoction within two minutes. Even though she felt a little silly drinking from the oversize, ornate glass, complete with straw and paper umbrella, Lauren had to admit the tropical drink was delicious.

"Blackberry liqueur, cranberry juice, and rum."

"What?" Cassie's voice pulled Lauren from her thoughts, which had unwittingly returned to her troubles.

Cassie scowled at her. "You were a million miles away. Cut it out and have fun. You promised, remember?"

"I'm sorry. What were you saying about blackberries?"

Her sister rolled her eyes and held up her drink. "Blackberry liqueur, cranberry juice, and rum. Mitch said they were the secret ingredients."

"Mitch?"

"Our waiter." Cassie pointed behind Lauren, toward the bar. "He's gorgeous. And if you didn't notice him, then I'm truly worried about you."

Lauren turned, but she didn't see Mitch. Her gaze had stopped on the figure who filled the entranceway, his black hair reflecting the neon light of the shamrock that blinked above him.

"Jesse," she whispered.

"What?"

Lauren quickly covered her reaction by pretending to ogle the waiter. "I said, you're right. He is gorgeous." It would never do to let her sister know that Jesse McCain was there. Cassie was already convinced romance was budding between them and no doubt would embarrass her beyond belief.

She lowered her head to sip from her drink, relieved

that Jesse hadn't noticed her. She watched as he wove his way through the crowd at the bar, eventually cutting a path through the couples on the dance floor rather than maneuver his way past the closely spaced tables. Tilting her head to get a better look, she saw him join a burly-looking man and two very pretty, very provocatively dressed women.

So that was Jesse McCain's type. An unexpected heat filled her face and stung her eyes. It figured.

"Hey, party animal, take it easy on that drink or I'll have to peel you up off the floor."

Lauren lifted her head at her sister's voice, surprised to see more than half of the icy drink had disappeared. She fanned her face with a laminated menu. "Yeah, you're right. I'm not much of a drinker. And on top of that, I'm hungry."

Cassie was more than happy to summon Mitch back to take their order. Lauren had just requested the restaurant's biggest steak and shrimp combination when she felt someone move behind her.

"Still making up for yesterday?" The voice was smooth and low, little more than a whisper. She knew without looking that it was Jesse. He was so close, his warm breath lifted the delicate hairs on the back of her exposed neck. Goose bumps flowed across her arms in a warm wave.

When she turned to look at him, she found him leaning against the back of her chair. "Oh . . . h-hi," she stammered.

"Do you plan on eating that whole order all by yourself, or are you sharing it with someone?" He nodded toward the empty chair between the sisters.

Lauren had the strangest urge to fabricate a date.

"No. I mean yes. Like you said, I'm making up for lost time."

He straightened, looking even taller and more imposing as she stared up at him. He held out his hand to her. "Dance with me."

Lauren felt her shoulders tighten at the suggestion. Dancing meant touching. A shiver ran up her spine at the thought of Jesse's strong hands holding her. The truth was, she didn't trust herself around him. "I can't. My steak . . ."

"It won't arrive for quite a while, judging by the size of the crowd here tonight."

"But my sister . . ." Lauren motioned toward Cassie.

Cassie only looked amused as she met Jesse's eyes. "I don't mind." She gave Lauren a self-satisfied smile.

Lauren felt a sense of panic as she glanced at the other couples on the dance floor, swaying sensually to the slow beat. She shook her head, but when she opened her mouth to offer another excuse, she couldn't think of anything to say.

"Let's call a truce." He gently grasped the underside of her arm, tugging her to her feet.

She allowed herself to be pulled onto the dance floor, which up close seemed no larger than a postage stamp. All her rational thoughts shattered as Jesse's hand trailed down her arm, his fingers weaving through her own. His fingers were warm and strong, hardened by rough work, and the palm of her hand was instantly pierced with a sensual ache as his skin slid against hers. Her heart pounded, her thoughts grew foggy.

She smoothed an escaped tendril of hair from her forehead as he turned to take her in his arms. "Are you sure your girlfriend won't mind?" she asked. As soon as the words were out, she was dying to take them back.

Jesse's mouth curved into an amused grin. "So, you knew I was here," he said bluntly.

"I, uh . . . thought I saw you come in." She took a step toward him to cover her embarrassment.

He finished eliminating the distance between them, and before she had time to react, he pulled her to him in an intimate embrace. She stumbled, more intoxicated from the feel of his hands against her back than from the liquor she'd drunk.

She leaned back to look him in the face. "Those tropical drinks they make here pack quite a punch. I'm afraid I drank mine too fast."

He drew her against him again, and Lauren was forced to brace her hands on his chest to steady herself. She thought she heard his breathing quicken before he lowered his mouth to her ear.

"Be careful or you might get light-headed."

Light-headed was exactly what she was feeling. Every nerve ending in her body was screaming for her to get closer to Jesse McCain, and the effects of her drink weren't helping. She struggled to remember why she was angry with him.

"So, you saw me but you weren't going to say hello?" He moved his hands in a slow circle against the small of her back, and she had to repeat his question in her head before she could answer. And the safest answer, she decided, was to change the subject.

"Do you and your friends come here often?" She gestured toward the table.

Jesse cocked his head. "That's Ken Lowell, a friend of mine. Yeah, we either come here or go to some other bar in some other town just like it." He met her curious stare. "Ken and I are kindred, nomadic souls, I suppose. We've worked together for the last ten years and known each other even longer." He chuckled. "Forever, actually."

Lauren couldn't help but notice the odd, somewhat sad expression that crossed his face. "Forever?"

He sighed and pulled her a little closer. "It seems like forever. We've known each other since we were teenagers." Jesse smiled his crooked smile. "Ken was the only kid in my high school with a home life worse than mine, so we became friends."

She had a thousand questions. Suddenly she wanted to know everything about Jesse McCain, but the look on his face told her he'd tell her only what he wanted her to know.

"We were old enough to know we were trapped," he went on, "and too young to do anything about it." He shrugged. "So when things got bad, we'd take off together. We used to walk the fields near the railroad tracks looking for something to get into."

"What did you find?"

"Nothing really. Just the things boys find interesting when girls aren't around—arrowheads, a patch of rabbit tobacco . . . Escape, mostly."

Lauren cut her eyes toward Ken, seeing the laughing, seemingly carefree man in a new light. "At least you had each other."

"You're right. We got an apartment together and part-time jobs as soon as we graduated from high school. Since neither of us seemed ready to quit poking around in the dirt, we enrolled in the same classes in college and ended up in the same field—literally." Jesse laughed softly. "Hell, now I think we're stuck with each other."

His hands returned to stroking her back, and Lauren sensed that the window to his past had just closed.

"You still didn't answer my question," he said, proving her right. "You weren't going to say hello tonight?"

She tried to ignore the tingling sensation that vibrated up her spine as he slid her silk shirt against her skin. "We didn't exactly part on good terms yesterday," she finally said.

He abruptly stopped dancing, holding her away from him to look into her eyes. "Lauren, I know how upset you are about the freeway proposal, but I'm not to blame."

She stared into his face, mesmerized by the warm highlights in his brown eyes. As she looked into those eyes she felt a sense of belonging, and she grew cold from the lack of his embrace.

I want him to hold me. A tremor of panic rushed through her at the thought. He's part of the system, Lauren, she reminded herself. Don't be naive. His boyish grin was nothing but a calculated public relations scheme, the light of desire in his eyes all too typically male. Where would Jesse McCain be when the chips were down? She doubted he knew, doubted he cared.

She squared her shoulders. "You should have told me you were the only one assigned to the excavation. You lied to me."

"No, you assumed something that wasn't true." His voice was low and soothing.

She noted the strong lines of his jaw, the high cheekbones that accentuated a predator's eyes. The warmth that radiated from his body reminded her that tonight he had selected her as his prey.

The music changed to a fast song and their standoff abruptly ended. Lauren wasn't sure whether she felt disappointment or relief.

Jesse put his arm around her shoulders and lightened the mood with a lazy smile. "Come and meet Ken. He's a worthless womanizer, but he's a good friend."

As they approached the table, Lauren saw Ken was wearing a puzzled expression, which looked a little comical on such a brawny, masculine face. She smiled in the direction of the two women with him, but was met with icy stares.

"Ken," Jesse said, "I'd like you to meet Lauren Adams."

Ken's expression went from curious to entertained. "Lauren Adams from the Adams property you're excavating, I take it?"

"Yes," Lauren answered, and moved to shake his hand.

"No, no, don't do that." Jesse pulled her back. "He bites," he added, and grinned.

The redhead next to Ken crossed her legs, baring a long expanse of white thigh. "What a coincidence." She paused until Lauren made eye contact with her. "So do I."

Ken cleared his throat. "This is Penny."

There was an awkward silence, and Lauren looked at Jesse.

"And this is . . ." Jesse gestured toward the brunette who was looking quite perturbed. "I'm sorry, I don't remember your name."

"Sherry." The woman took a long drag on her cigarette and stared wordlessly at Lauren.

Lauren doubted there was a way to make polite conversation with the women, so she didn't try. Besides, her mind was reeling with the knowledge that Jesse was alone tonight after all. She knew it wasn't logical, but with the jealous look on the other woman's face and Jesse's arm draped possessively around her, Lauren felt more alive than she had in years. She knew she couldn't let it continue, but for the moment she was going to enjoy herself.

"Ken and I just met here for a beer," Jesse said to her. "I missed a staff meeting yesterday and he's agreed to bring me up to speed."

Lauren felt a pang of guilt. "Did you miss the meeting because of me?"

He winked at her. "It was worth it." Behind her, one of the women snorted and Jesse shot her a warning look. "Speaking of yesterday, did I leave my map at your place?"

"Yes." Lauren blushed as she recalled the ugly scene when she had knocked the map from Jesse's hands. "As a matter of fact, I brought it tonight to show to my sister. . . ." Her voice trailed off as she realized she'd left Cassie alone. "She's probably wondering where I am."

"I'm not so sure about that." Jesse sounded amused.

When she looked over her shoulder, she found that Mitch had shed his waiter's apron and was sitting in her chair.

"Well, maybe not." She bit her lip. "The map is in her car. I'll get it for you."

"We were just about to head over to Ken's apartment to go over the meeting notes. I'll walk out with you."

Lauren wanted to avoid a lengthy conversation about Jesse, so she crept up behind Cassie, winked at Mitch, and slipped the car keys from the outside pocket of her sister's purse, which she had carelessly slung over the back of her chair.

Jesse was waiting for her at the door of the restaurant. "Are you always so devious?"

She waved her hand. "Believe me, if you knew my sister, you'd thank me."

As they walked to the car, Lauren could easily imagine that they'd been on a date. It was a perfect summer night. The sun had warmed the grasses and flowers until they'd released their scent, and a cool, fragrant wind had sprung up the minute the sun had dipped below the horizon.

She suppressed the crazy urge to slip her hand into Jesse's. If they had been on a date tonight, where would they go now? Back to his place? She wondered where a man like Jesse McCain lived. A messy bachelor's apartment, a sprawling country house, an ultramodern condo? Would he want to make love to her?

At the thought of making love to Jesse, a knot of longing tightened in her abdomen. She believed she'd outgrown that kind of naive passion, but Jesse turned her to butter every time he touched her—no matter how innocently. She shook her head. She had to put a stop to this. Even if he was interested in her, she couldn't get involved. She needed his alliance, maybe even his sympathy, if he was going to be of any help to her, but she didn't have the energy for a romance right now.

Besides, she'd jumped in way too fast with Roger. And, at least at the outset, he'd appeared more stable than Jesse McCain could even dream of being. But he'd turned out to be the wrong man entirely. In Roger's book the word "divorced" was synonymous with "almost divorced."

Lauren was surprised to feel her fingernails biting into the palms of her hands. She forced herself to relax, though Cassie's mention of her thirtieth birthday didn't help. No, if she was going to bother dating at all, from now on it would be the right kind of man. Not the kind who had one foot on the next flight out of town, like Jesse McCain.

She was annoyed to find her hand trembling as she inserted the key into the door of Cassie's car. "I think I tossed it in the back," she muttered as she switched on the overhead light and leaned across the console. A few seconds later she flipped off the light and emerged with the map.

"Thanks." Jesse tugged it from her hand while she fumbled to relock the car door.

She'd barely pivoted when Jesse circled her waist with his arms. The map tumbled to the asphalt as he pinned her against the car with his body.

His warm hands branded her flesh straight through the cool silk of her shirt. Hadn't she known from the very beginning that he would touch her like this someday? Hadn't she wanted him to?

He stood still, not even seeming to breath. She knew he was giving her one last chance to object, to sever the bond of desire that was pulling them to each other.

His eyes narrowed as he studied her face. She thought she saw a satisfied smile brush his lips as he ran his hands up her sides, his thumbs finally coming to rest against the sides of her breasts.

Lauren's breath caught in her chest, every nerve ending contracting at the boldness of his touch.

"You tempt me," he whispered.

"I didn't know. . . ."

He took a deep breath between clenched teeth. "Yes you did. You knew from the first moment."

His muscular thigh moved to part her legs, and she felt his arousal pressing against her. Her thin silk trousers slid over her skin, and she thought she'd cry out with pleasure. Catching her lower lip between her teeth, she tried in vain to control the wave of desire that washed over her.

Jesse tilted her chin up until she met his eyes. The primal desire she saw there shocked her. She didn't need this. It was all wrong. He was all wrong. She should tell him to stop while she still could.

His lips parted, and he massaged the swollen edge of his lower lip with his tongue. It was a small move—he probably wasn't even aware that he'd done it—but it sent the need in her soaring. She shut her eyes. Her problems suddenly seemed insignificant. It was true. She wanted him to kiss her. Wanted it more than anything.

He lowered his head until his lips found hers, feather-light and trembling. Still she felt the raw hunger beneath his control. He withdrew, then returned to wet her lower lip with his tongue, and she met his teasing with her own.

Jesse's mouth was on hers then, urging more response from her with each dip of his tongue. A hunger like she'd never known rose up to meet his, and her hips instinctively sought his. Rough denim met silk as he grasped her hips, matching her need with his own.

A low moan echoed in the back of his throat as he

pulled the clasp from her hair. His hands tangled in the loose strands, pulling her head back to allow him more access to her mouth and neck.

From the recesses of her brain, she heard a car start. Jesse lifted his head and pulled slightly away from her. No, she thought. She wanted his lips on hers, wanted to return to the ecstasy she felt with their bodies pressed against each other.

As the passion-induced haze cleared from her mind, though, she realized the interruption was the life ring she needed to cling to, the one thing that might keep her from drowning in her irrational desire for Jesse McCain. It could never work between them, even if he was interested in something more than a passing affair.

"I can't do this." She blurted out the words before she lost her nerve.

Jesse's eyes darkened as they searched her face. He looked more than angry; he looked dangerous. He slowly lowered his hips back to hers, and brushed his knuckles against her hardened nipple with lazy thoroughness. "It feels like you could to me."

She tried to suppress a tremor of desire, but failed. "I want to be friends. . . ."

"Oh God, not that line!" He released her and fell against the car in mock defeat.

Again, she instantly wanted him back, wanted to feel his body pressed to hers. Why was she depriving herself of the pleasure she was certain he could bring her? Because it couldn't last, she reminded herself.

She took a steadying breath. "You have a job that could take you halfway around the world tomorrow. I'm a homebody. You're a—"

He laced his fingers through hers and singed her

with a piercing gaze. "You don't know what I am. What I want."

She felt her resolve falter at the warmth of his fingers entwined with hers. "But I know myself, Jesse. There are things I want one day. I've made some tough decisions lately. Like not dating just for the sake of dating."

A shadow crossed his features, masking the affection and desire she had seen there just moments earlier. "You mean not dating just for sex."

"Yes." She was both shocked and relieved that he'd put it into words.

He kissed her without warning, a passion-filled, angry kiss that left her craving the taste of him. She felt a desperation for something, but she wasn't sure if it was his desperation or hers.

"I'm not sure I can be just friends, Lauren." He ran a callused finger across her trembling lower lip. "Are you?"

She nodded, hoping she looked more convincing than she felt.

"Okay then." He cupped the side of her face for a moment before he retrieved the map from the ground and walked to his Jeep.

Lauren watched him go. Her hands, her entire body, were shaking. She could deny it all she wanted, but her body had betrayed her. Betrayed her with the truth. There had never been anyone like Jesse McCain. And she knew there never would be again.

Lauren felt like a ghost as she drifted back into the Green Shamrock. She spotted Cassie dancing with Mitch and was relieved to have a moment to herself. She took her compact out of her purse and was applying a new coat of lipstick when Cassie returned to the table.

"Your hair!" she said. "What happened?"

Lauren brushed it out with her fingers. "Oh, you know how easily it comes down."

"Yeah, and I was born yesterday." Cassie nodded toward the door, smiling. "Who is he, anyway?"

Lauren looked over her shoulder to find Jesse had returned and was watching her from the doorway. His eyes bored into hers, eliminating the space that separated them. Her heart leaped in her chest. Had he come back for her, seen through her words after all?

Instead, he gave a small wave as Ken joined him, then the two slipped out the door and into the shadows of the night.

Lauren faced Cassie again.

"That," she answered, "was Jesse McCain."

FOUR

Jesse swallowed the last of his coffee as he drove, then tossed the cardboard cup into the crumpled fast-food sack. He loved his job, but Mondays were still a drag. As he turned onto the single-lane dirt road that led to Lauren's house, he wondered if he'd see her, and if so what mood he'd find her in.

The first time he'd met her, she had been as mad as a cornered bobcat. The second time she'd needed him, and the vulnerable woman he had held in his arms two nights earlier had left him with an aching need like no other woman ever had.

He downshifted as the Jeep rocked on the rutted country road that began the descent into the valley. And now Lauren Adams wanted to be his friend. He laughed out loud. He'd always heard the cliché, but frankly it had never been said to him.

Even as an adolescent, he'd had his share of willing females. He suspected they'd been drawn more to his pain than to him. Some maternal drive to make things better. He wadded the paper sack into a ball, crushing the scraps of biscuit and the Styrofoam cup inside, and threw it into the empty passenger's seat.

Maybe those women had made things better for him, at least to some extent. Lord knows he had been searching for something all his life—some permanent form of happiness. His father had been too busy chasing the next executive level to notice him, and his mother had been too busy packing their things and crying into a liquor bottle.

Jesse shook his head and looked at his watch. Six-thirty A.M. Too damned early to be dredging up the past.

The sun was already burning the mist from the creek bank as he turned onto Lauren's gravel driveway. Her dog ran to meet him, yipping a bark that was more a greeting than a threat. Then he noticed her.

She was sitting on the front steps of the sprawling old farmhouse. He felt her gaze on him as he pulled to a stop in the driveway. He checked his watch again. What the hell was she doing up at this time of day?

Before he could get out, she was standing at the passenger door, her fingers curled over the partially opened window.

"I'm going with you," she said bluntly. "And don't bother saying no."

"You're going with me?" he repeated, stunned.

She set an oversize thermos and a backpack on the hood of the Jeep and opened the door. Cocking her hip against the empty seat, she lifted the map from the console and unrolled it. "Where do you plan on starting?"

He stared at her profile as she scanned the map. Her long lashes and aristocratic nose could have given her prettiness a snobbish air, but her simple long-sleeved T-shirt and worn blue jeans quelled that danger. She had French-braided her hair, but already honey-blond wisps were straying toward her face. One strand had settled against her lower lip, caught in the dewy lip gloss she wore. Jesse was captivated by that strand, envied its freedom to settle itself against her softest skin.

If she was so damned determined to keep their relationship platonic, there was no way he could allow her to go with him, not if he had to look at that strand of hair playing against her mouth all day long.

"*I* was planning on doing a shovel test at as many of the excavation sites as I can get to, but you're not—"

"Don't even start, Jesse, because I'm going." She thrust her chin toward him. He would have laughed at that delicate chin so set with determination, but the hint of a well-thought-out counterattack glimmered in her eyes.

"You don't think I'm going to do my job, do you?" he asked.

A guilty expression crossed her face before she replaced it with a determined scowl.

Of course she didn't trust him, he thought. And why should she? He hadn't, couldn't, tell her the truth. Jesse lowered his voice. "Lauren, I'm going to do my job. Why else would I be parading around at this obscene time of day?"

"I never said I didn't trust you to do your job. For your information, I was planning on assisting you, not monitoring you."

Her expression, her entire self, exuded a strength he couldn't help but admire. He wanted her to come with him. Hell, he wanted *her*.

He took the map from her hands and allowed it to

recoil. "You wouldn't know where to start," he said, more gruffly than he intended.

"I know how to carry a shovel, and I know everything there is to know about this land."

"Look, I was going to start way up at Turtle Creek. Why don't you let me work my way back, and when I get a little closer to your place, you can watch."

"Don't patronize me. This may be all fun and games to you, but it's everything to me." Anger sparked in her blue eyes before she set her expression again. "I don't understand why you're resisting this so much."

Every minute he stared into her trusting face, Jesse was less certain himself. There was a time when he would have confided in her without hesitation. Every instinct he had told him Lauren Adams was as trustworthy as they came. Would it kill him to find out, to spend enough time with her to make a decision based on his gut, instead of the caustic cynicism he had carried with him since the Coosa excavation?

True, the excavation had been a personal and all-too-public failure. He had pushed for it, placed both his and Luke Ebsin's reputations on the line—all because he had been so cocksure he knew where the elusive Coosa chiefdom was located. Yes, it had backfired, and he'd played it safe ever since.

He hated playing it safe. But he'd vowed not to take any more chances until Luke Ebsin was no longer under scrutiny. And that was a vow he intended to keep.

"Admit it, Jesse, it'll go faster if you have some help."

A gentle breeze lifted the wisps of hair that had escaped her braid, surrounding her face in an angelic frame. Jesse ground his teeth in frustration. He was damned by his own conscience either way.

In the end he wasn't sure if right or wrong won out, but he satisfied his own growing need to have Lauren near him. "You'll have a heatstroke in that long-sleeved shirt and blue jeans."

She laughed, a sparkling, sincere laugh that made his heart clutch. "And you'll have such a case of chiggers and mosquito bites in those shorts that you'll wish you'd become an accountant instead."

He reached below the seat of the Jeep and retrieved a can of insect repellent. "Never leave home without it."

She smiled. "I didn't. But I prefer not to flaunt the goods in front of the enemy."

He allowed his gaze to flow over her body, taking his time despite the nervous squirm she gave. When he looked up, she was leaning toward him, though he was sure she didn't realize it. "I suddenly regret that you feel that way."

He expected her to pretend not to catch his meaning, but she surprised him. "I've already told you, I don't think you're the enemy."

He brushed the strand of hair from her mouth, despite his resolve to ignore it. "Yeah, yeah, I know. Friends."

"Right."

"Okay, friend, this time you're right. I could use some help." He took a moment to relish the shocked look that crossed her face. So far, she'd been the one to surprise him. "Let's get started before it gets too hot."

He slid out of the Jeep and walked around to unlock the cargo area. He felt her presence as she moved to stand behind him. His body stirred. It was the same feeling of awareness he had when someone was staring at him, only more intense and so sexually arousing, it disturbed him. What was the problem? He had been attracted to the opposite sex for a good twenty years.

He lifted the hatchback, forcing her to step back, and he felt the loss of her warmth as keenly as if he'd plunged into the creek. What made her different from other women he'd wanted to go to bed with? It was probably just the challenge, he told himself. After all, she had made it clear she wasn't interested.

"I'll get that." She reached toward a collapsible aluminum shovel.

Jesse lifted the shovel from the cargo area, holding on to it as her slender fingers wrapped around the handle. When he didn't let go, she looked up at him. He studied her heart-shaped face, his gaze focusing on her full mouth before he met her eyes again. He smiled. Her eyes were a lighter blue, a more brilliant blue, than they had been moments before. She glanced away from him as she tugged the shovel from his grip.

Her words may have declared one intention, but her body was whispering another. He could use that to his advantage in the days to come, and he doubted she'd be able to hold out for long. Oddly, he didn't find that thought appealing. Oh, the physical part appealed to him. It was just that he wanted her to admit to herself first that she wanted him.

He grabbed a green canvas bag, the pit of its large belly filled to capacity with equipment. He had planned on slipping the shovel inside it, too, but Lauren would likely accuse him of patronizing her again if she didn't have something to carry. He narrowed his eyes at her backpack lying on the hood of his Jeep. By the time she hauled it, the shovel, and her ridiculously large thermos up the bluff that led to the mouth of Turtle Creek, her little experiment in archaeology would be over. And doubtless he'd be to blame for any bumps and bruises she acquired along the way.

"Let's go, partner." He closed the hatchback with a thud.

They fell into a silent rhythm as they crossed the open meadow adjoining Lauren's pasture, the only sounds being the swish of lanky summer weeds that brushed against their legs, and the cry of a red-tailed hawk as it circled overhead. Jesse's shoulder was already feeling the weight of his bag when they finally reached the thicket of woods on the other side.

"The old logging road is to the left." Lauren moved ahead of him to take the lead.

That was fine with him. The road was barely discernible beneath the heavy underbrush. He was impressed with the confident way she picked the best route around fallen trees, and appreciated her pointing toward any low-hanging spiderwebs, complete with fat spiders, that he would otherwise have walked straight into. And they were making great time. He grimaced, however, when she began to climb a steep hill ahead of him and a flash of clean, unmarred buckskin caught his eye.

Lauren had tucked the cuffs of her jeans into her hiking boots and bound the denim to the leather with masking tape. He admired her attempt to ward off ticks and the thorny underbrush, but the most damning fact remained the same. The boots were new. Just-off-the-shelf new.

"Mind if I take the lead for a while?"

She stopped and looked over her shoulder, brushing

back the strands of white-gold that lay against her now-moist forehead. "I'm fine."

He threw his head back and laughed. "Yes, you are. Believe me, from the angle I'm at . . ." He used his most lecherous stare and fixed his gaze on her perky little butt.

Her eyes darkened to a dangerous shade of navy. "Be my guest," she snapped, pointing the shovel in front of her.

Well, it hadn't earned him any feathers in his cap, but at least he had the lead without argument. And the ability to slow the pace before she bloodied her feet in the new boots.

If he had thought Lauren was in a quiet mood before, he was wrong. Now he didn't even hear her breathing. He stopped when the logging road reached Turtle Creek, unable to stand the frosty silence any longer.

"Break time," he announced without looking at her, and tossed the heavy canvas bag to the ground. He unzipped it and pulled out a worn blue tarp, which he spread out at the bank of the creek. He weighted one end down with the canvas bag and sat down on the other with a sigh. Lauren stood frozen a few feet away.

"Come sit down, Lauren. I'm not going to bite." Her eyebrows shot up, and she stared at him as if she didn't believe a word of what he was saying. "Lighten up, will you? I was just kidding with you back there."

She sat down between him and the canvas bag, her body rigid with tension. He took the shovel from her hand and tossed it to one side, but when he moved to help her out of her backpack, she shot him a warning look.

"Do you want to strain your back and bloody your feet at the same time?" he asked.

Her head snapped around. "What are you talking about?"

He tugged the backpack from her shoulders. "I'm talking about those price-tag-new boots of yours. We've been walking for miles and have quite a few more to go. I had you pegged as brighter than that."

She looked down at her feet, as if she were considering something more. "They feel fine," she said finally.

"Yeah, now they do." He grunted. "You should probably turn back."

"No!" Her loud voice was jarring in their quiet, peaceful surroundings, and the crystal sound of the creek's flow punctuated the silence that followed.

"Well, at least take your boots off and soak your feet in the water for a few minutes."

"I said they're okay."

"Soak your feet or *I'm* turning back."

She ripped the masking tape from her ankles without a word, but the anger that radiated from her body was so hot that Jesse could almost see the red. She mumbled something under her breath as she fumbled with the leather laces of her boots.

"What did you say?"

"I *said* you're all a bunch of damned control freaks, that's what I said."

He stifled a laugh at her foul language. "And just who else belongs to this lofty group of people you're lumping me in with, Lauren?"

She stood, hopping on one foot as she tugged her right boot off. "Men. All men!"

"Oh."

She threw her boot onto the tarp, grazing his left shoulder with it. So, he thought as he rubbed the scratch, this was it. He was about to discover why she was so determined to keep him at arm's length.

Her left boot hit the tarp with a resounding thud, dangerously close to his right knee. He watched as she sat down and rolled up the cuff of her jeans, revealing a shapely ankle. Her skin flashed white against the backdrop of the murky green water, and the tangled honeysuckle and wild fern that grew from the fertile soil of the bank. His breath caught in his chest.

She was a lady, and yet no lady had ever turned him on like this. Maybe that was just it. There was something more to her, something earthy and basic but with a passion, like the temper he'd just experienced, lying beneath the surface. He had a feeling that when he unearthed it, it would be the greatest discovery he'd ever made.

It dawned on him then that he had always shied away from women like her. He picked up her boot and stroked the fresh buckskin. No, the kind of women he sought out—or that sought him out—were the ones who appreciated him for what he was, what he'd been all his life: Temporary.

"So we're all a bunch of no-good control freaks, huh?"

No answer.

Still, he was curious. Something, or more likely someone, had caused Lauren to wall herself away from men, from romance. She walked to the creek bank, sat down on the edge of the tarp, and dunked her feet in the water. No hesitation, he noticed. How sweet it would be if she would give herself to him that way.

"Who was he, Lauren?"

She turned her head in his direction, but didn't make eye contact. "What are you talking about?"

He was surprised at the sincerely puzzled tone to her voice. "Someone hurt you. Who was he?"

She laughed. "You're giving my love life way too much credit."

"No, a woman like you wouldn't be alone unless it was her choice."

"Maybe it is."

"And maybe there's a reason for it." He held his breath, knowing he was pushing too hard.

"Look, if you want to blame someone for my sorry attitude toward men, you can credit the pack of wolves I used to work with. And maybe my own poor judgment."

He felt an odd mix of relief and unsatisfied curiosity. "That still doesn't answer my question."

Her shoulders tensed under her shirt. "Which is?"

"Which is, who was in your life before me?" His own words echoed in his head, and Jesse ran his hand through his unbound hair to cover his shock. Did he really consider himself in her life?

"Well, let's see, there was Bobby Brockman in the sixth grade."

He laughed, relieved that she didn't try to pin down any meaning to his words, though he doubted she'd missed the slip.

She went on. "If you need some scoundrel to blame my animosity toward the opposite sex on, my ex-boss—make that my ex-boyfriend as well—would fit the bill." She flipped a broken twig into the swift current of the creek. "Roger and I were seeing each other . . ."

When she didn't continue, Jesse took a chance. "I guess it wasn't 'married and happily ever after,' then?"

She laughed. "Try *already* married."

Jesse felt the fine hairs on the back of his neck rise, and an illogical anger consumed him. It was one thing to assume there was some painful episode in her past. Now, though, he had a name, and he had a reason to hate the man: He'd hurt Lauren, deceiving her in a shameful way.

Suddenly she stood and walked over to him, sitting down next to him. She retrieved her socks and tugged her boot from his hand, then shoved one thick sports sock onto her damp foot. Jesse fished around behind him until he came up with her second boot, and handed it to her.

She sat the boot beside her other one, her long fingers toying with the thick leather laces. "It wasn't so bad for me." She shook her head. "He had kids."

Jesse balled his hands into fists. "Lauren, I'm sorry."

"I know I've got quite a chip on my shoulder when it comes to men in authority, but Roger isn't to blame for all of it."

"What then?"

She leaned back on her elbows and looked up at the patch of azure sky that peeked through the thick foliage above them. "It's hard to explain. It was years' worth of frustration in the business world, the glass ceiling and all the mental torture that goes with it." She shut her eyes. "Maybe I wasn't cut out for it. I didn't play games and I didn't sleep around." She chuckled. "I even had one female coworker tell me that I just didn't get it."

"So you quit your job to open the stable."

She nodded. "But not right away. Funny thing, it's always been my dream. I just didn't realize it until my parents moved away." She met Jesse's puzzled look. "My father was an engineer, so I became an engineer. I thought I was happy, but it turns out I didn't love my job half as much as I loved pleasing my father."

Jesse suddenly felt the weight of her decision, and her fear. All he had to do was tell her. Tell her that the other route had been chosen for the interchange, that her home wasn't at risk. Hell, there was no reason for her even to be with him now—in the middle of nowhere, blistering her feet in her determination to help him. No, he corrected himself, in her determination to help him help her. God, had anyone ever trusted him like that? Even though her home wasn't in danger, he had the disconcerting feeling that he would be if—or rather when—she learned the truth.

She straightened, pulling her legs to her chest and hugging them. "I thought that from now on I would be the only one controlling what happened in my life." She lifted up a shiny green oak leaf that had drifted down from the umbrella of leaves above them. "And then the state stepped in." She began plucking at the edges of the leaf, tearing the membrane away from the skeleton. "I'm sick to death of men who think it's their job to control the world, no matter what the cost to others."

Jesse stifled a laugh. "Well don't look at me, Lauren. I have enough trouble controlling my own world."

Hell, all he'd ever wanted was to feel like he had command of his own life—and it had been spinning out of control since he was a child. But now he saw himself through her eyes, felt her fear, and felt a dangerous new loyalty emerging. A loyalty to Lauren.

She stopped toying with the leaf. "And what about a man like you? Are you alone?"

He moaned, wishing he could avoid the question. But turnabout was fair play, and there was an undeniable determiniation in her eyes. "I'm a whole different ball game, Lauren."

She cocked her head, and the expression on her face told him there was no escape. "How so?"

He stretched his legs out on the tarp with what he hoped would be enough indifference to end the conversation. "Let's just say that with me, being alone is learned behavior."

"What do you mean?"

Obviously, avoiding the question was going to be impossible. "My childhood wasn't like other people's." He shook his head. "I didn't grow up, I survived."

He heard Lauren's body shift against the plastic tarp, but didn't look. He wanted to avoid the pity he knew he'd see in her eyes.

"We moved around a lot," he continued. "Whenever we stayed in one place long enough for me to connect with anybody, it was only a matter of time—" He shrugged. "So I didn't make connections, except for Ken." He hesitated a moment before he met her gaze. "I guess I still don't."

As he looked at her, he was assaulted by the mixture of compassion—not pity—and promise that played across her face. She was beautiful, and the look in her eyes told him she could care about him as no other woman ever had.

She was honest. He was deceiving her. But at that moment he knew he couldn't stop himself from touching her.

He tugged the now barren leaf from her hand and eased her fingers apart with his own. Her eyes met his, wide with anticipation, and he brushed her knuckles with the tips of his fingers until her hand softened against his.

He let his gaze drift to her mouth, dewy pink and softly parted. It was a mistake. He felt every muscle in his body tense, and almost moaned out loud at the bittersweet ache that filled his loins.

The heat from the contact of their hands leaped like a fire up his arm and ignited the rest of his body, and he thought he'd burst into flames if he couldn't taste her lips, feel her cool, sweet mouth against his.

She started to speak, but it was too late to hear as he covered her lips with his own. The pleasure of her kiss, her tongue meeting his, gave him a surreal sense of completeness. He lowered her to the tarp and was atop her so quickly, it startled even him.

A voice in his head whispered to slow down, but he pressed his hips against hers instead, a burst of lightning-raw pleasure striking him at the contact. If the world had opened up and swallowed them, he wouldn't have noticed. Not as long as Lauren's soft body was beneath him. He lowered his chest to brush against hers, and experienced a surge of male possessiveness to find her nipples as hard and erect as he was.

She's mine. The words echoed inside his head, barely penetrating the desire that flooded his brain. He felt her hand on his shoulder, and expected her to push him away. Instead she slid her hand across the back of his neck and pulled him down to her. His blood careened wildly through his body. Could she hear how loudly his heart was beating?

He had kissed her before, but this was different. This was a perfect blending of both their passions. The feel of her lips, her tongue against his, intensified the pounding in his ears to a roar. Her mouth fit so perfectly against his. He pulled back, stroking his tongue against the inside of her lip. God, if their bodies fit together this perfectly . . .

He shifted his weight to free his right hand and jerked Lauren's shirt from the waistband of her jeans. His hands were hungry for the feel of her skin, and his palms ached to cup her breasts. He held his breath, willing himself to slow down.

He shut his eyes with pleasure as he eased his hands up her bare rib cage, relishing the silky warmth of her skin. A small smile formed as he encountered a lace-edged scrap of silk attached to the delicate underwire of her bra. He'd seen such sexy underthings discarded in the corner of her bathroom. He had pictured her in them—how many times?—since that night. Only one thing had bothered him then, and now he knew. They hadn't been worn for a special occasion, or for some special man.

Unbelievably, he felt himself grow harder at that thought.

He opened his eyes to find that Lauren had closed hers, one arm thrown above her head. He'd never seen a more beautiful woman, he thought. But it was the sensual expression on her face that almost pushed him over the edge. Her lips were full and moist, and her hair had almost freed itself entirely from her braid, the honey-blond strands spread wildly across the tarp.

Even before he'd finished pushing her bra out of the way, he was lowering his head to her breasts. Jesse felt as if he would burst as he tasted the salty V between her breasts. His thumb dipped below the silk of her bra, freeing one rosy nipple, then the other.

He allowed himself to admire the beauty of her breasts before he dipped his head, taking one tender crest into his mouth.

"I want to make love to you." He hadn't planned on making love to her, at least not there and then. But the words were hovering between them.

Her hands, which had been stroking his back, stilled. She opened her eyes. "Jesse . . ."

Her hesitation was just what he needed, and he took the opportunity to lavish the same tender treatment on her other breast. But as his mouth found the sensitive flesh of her nipple, her hand moved to the side of his jaw, her body stiffening.

"Jesse, wait . . ." She pushed gently against his face as she tried to wiggle up onto her elbows.

Every cell in his body rebelled against the command. He dipped his head again and gently suckled her nipple. He felt a shiver run through her, and when he finally pulled away, the fine hairs on his arms were standing on end.

He didn't want to hear what she had to say.

"What's wrong?" he finally whispered.

Her eyes bored into his, pleading for understanding. "We can't do this. We have to stop."

He heard the words, and he would heed them, but not yet. He brushed her lower lip with his thumb, then stroked it with his tongue. "You want to stop?"

"No. I mean yes." She pulled her shirt down, covering her breasts.

"I would rather stop a freight train right now." He looked away and laughed, but it was a strangled sound. "Only a fool would believe you still just want to be friends."

"And you're not a fool."

"I must be." He lifted the hem of her shirt and kissed the flesh next to her navel. "But only once. Next time . . ." He left a trail of kisses that ended at the waistband of her jeans. "Next time we won't stop."

"Yes we will."

The determination in her voice took him by surprise, and his eyes asked a question as their gazes locked.

Lauren looked away as she tugged her bra into place. "Because you'll leave," she whispered.

It took a moment for what she'd said to register. Then he felt as if he'd been kicked in the gut. He'd been on the move for so long, it had become a way of life. Still, he hadn't thought about leaving Lauren. In fact, it hadn't even occurred to him. That was a first. Hell, that was downright scary.

Lauren deserved someone who would be around. Someone who could be a husband, a father to her children. He looked down, staring without seeing, at the way the thin cotton of her shirt had molded itself to her flat stomach. For a moment he pictured her pregnant, her belly swollen with his growing child. A sweet ache filled him at the thought, a longing he hadn't even known existed. And it tied him in knots. He shook his head, unable to believe the trail his thoughts had taken.

"Jesse?"

He rolled to one side and pulled his knees to his chest, mentally cursing the pain of denial he knew he'd experience later. The hell of it was she wanted him as much as he did her. But he couldn't deny the truth of her words. "You're right," he said. "I'm sorry."

"No, I am." She reached out to touch his arm. "My

mind and my body are at war right now, and I'm not sure who just lost the battle."

When he looked up, he found her smiling at him, looking only slightly mortified at the awkwardness of the situation.

It took every ounce of strength he had to gather his composure, to give her the space she needed without making things more difficult. "You know what this means, don't you?"

"What?"

"Break is over."

He watched as she relaxed. Still, he couldn't let her dismiss too easily what had almost happened. Even though he knew it was cruel, knew she had changed her mind about making love for a damned good reason, he wanted her to experience the same ache of denial that he felt.

He leaned over her, commanding her to give up one last kiss before the spell was completely broken. He stroked one breast through her shirt, and felt a surge of satisfaction at the sharp intake of her breath. Reluctantly, he broke the kiss.

"Well, Lauren, you've definitely interfered with my concentration."

She bit her lower lip, then smiled a mischievous smile. "The creek would make a great substitute for a cold shower."

"Yeah?"

"I'm certain of it. You made me put my feet in, re-member?"

"I remember something to that effect."

She squirmed to a sitting position. "Throw me my backpack, will you?"

He passed it to her, noting with curiosity the smug look on her face. He understood as she pulled out a pair of well-worn running shoes.

"What the hell are those?" he asked.

"Tennis shoes."

Jesse stood, planting his hands on his hips. "I can see that. Why didn't you tell me you had them earlier?"

She pulled the laces on one shoe tight and produced a perfect bow before she answered. "You didn't ask. Besides, you were acting so superior that I didn't want to admit you were right."

"So you'd rather risk blisters than give me the satisfaction of being right?"

"No, I was just waiting until you forgot about it, until you were distracted or something before I slipped them on."

"Mission accomplished," he said with a smile.

Her eyes were twinkling with humor as she tugged on the other tennis shoe. Jesse's chest ached as intensely as other parts of his body. What was it about her that made him want to stay, to fix sandwiches in her kitchen and brush the hay from her hair? Whatever it was, it was the same thing that told him it was only a matter of time before he confessed the highway department's secrets. But not right now.

He pulled a rubber band from his pocket and bound his hair away from his face. Looking down, he found Lauren watching him. Desire lingered in her eyes before she replaced it with a smile. She held out her hand, and he pulled her to her feet, fighting the urge to draw her against him. Instead, he patted her bottom and pushed her away. He watched her saucy little behind as she trotted to the opposite corner of the tarp and began gathering it up without asking.

They folded the tarp silently, their actions in perfect sync. He rubbed his thumb against the alley that ran between his two bottom ribs, feeling a tightening in his gut that he wished he could ignore. No, now wasn't the time for confessions. Not after what had just passed between them.

Jesse stuffed the tarp back into the canvas bag, noticing for the first time how faded the bag had become over the years. As he hoisted the strap over his shoulder, he couldn't help but think it felt heavier. Well, he thought with a sour feeling in his stomach, guilt was a load he wasn't accustomed to carrying.

FIVE

The heat rising from the floor of the valley made the thick meadow grasses and clumps of blackberry bushes wave in a ghostly breeze that wasn't there. Lauren wiped her brow against her shirt sleeve. The wavering image of her barn in the distance added to the feeling of unreality as she forced one weary foot in front of the other.

She had to admit that she was as exhausted mentally as she was physically. How had things with Jesse gotten so out of hand so quickly? She replayed in her head the scene on the tarp, as she'd done all afternoon. What would have happened if her common sense hadn't intervened?

She shivered in the heat as she recalled the way Jesse had touched her, how he'd made her ache to feel him moving inside her. The whole thing couldn't have lasted more than a few minutes, but instinct told her she had been near the edge, near something wonderful that had passed her by before.

She fell in behind Jesse as their path through the overgrown field narrowed. She stared at his back, at the thick muscles that bunched around his shoulders, in contrast to his narrow waist and hips. A fresh surge of desire rushed through her as she watched the way his shorts pulled against the muscles in his upper legs and buttocks. She didn't doubt that he would be a great lover. No, would have been a great lover.

A lump formed in her throat as she realized that she had almost known him intimately when she really didn't know him at all.

She had nearly made a terrible mistake, one she wouldn't have been able to undo. As easy as it would be to give in to the temptation, making love with Jesse McCain would be disastrous. Her pulse danced as her mind conjured up an image of the two of them lying naked on the tarp, their bodies entwined. She shook her head. No, sex with someone who had no intention of sticking around wasn't her idea of smart, and she had gotten wise a long time ago when it came to men.

Finally, they reached the barbed wire fence that separated the overgrown meadow from Lauren's pasture. The short new grass on the other side of the fence would be a welcome relief. Since she had replaced her hiking boots with tennis shoes, her heavy gym socks had been assaulted by long-thorned brambles and cockleburs, leaving them bloodstained in more spots than she wanted to think about.

She stepped down on the center strand of barbed wire and tugged the top strand up as far as it would stretch, cursing softly as she pricked her finger on a barb.

"What was that?" Jesse sported an amused grin.

"Nothing. It's just that I hate this stuff. I'm going to replace it with board fencing just as soon as I can afford it." She leaned her head in the direction of the hole she had opened. "Go ahead and step through while I hold it."

Jesse looked as if he were about to say no, but then his grin widened. "A true gentleman would refuse, you know."

It was on the tip of her tongue to make a teasing remark about him not being a gentleman, until she recognized the trap. No, she wouldn't make a comment that referred even remotely to what had happened between them. That was territory she wasn't prepared to explore yet. Instead she just cocked an eyebrow, letting her expression speak for her.

Jesse smiled in her direction as he ducked between the sharp strands. "Is that a breeze or am I hallucinating?" he asked.

The stagnant late-afternoon air was beginning to stir, hinting that the heat wouldn't last, at least not into the night.

"I think I'd call that an almost-breeze." She stepped through the fence as Jesse held the strands apart for her. He didn't offer her his hand, and she felt a tug of regret. It was ridiculous, this game her mind was playing with her.

Jesse had been curiously quiet since the incident at the creek, although once they arrived at the Turtle Creek site he had seemed more at ease, explaining how he went about selecting the test sites and what clues he looked for. She realized how much he loved his job as she watched him probing and caressing the earth like a farmer who senses the riches the simple dirt will yield.

With her, however, he had been distant, professional. At times she'd found herself wishing he would touch her with the same tenderness he touched the soil, take her hand or kiss her again.

But he hadn't. Of course, it was better that way. She had made up her mind that she wouldn't respond if he did. She couldn't. Not when her future was at stake. She had to survive this crisis by being smart, taking action, and avoiding distractions. Especially the kind Jesse had to offer.

Yes, the last thing she needed right now was a broken heart and a wounded ego when Jesse left. And Jesse McCain would leave.

She felt her stomach knot with anxiety when they reached the Jeep. Jesse took the shovel and thermos from her, and set them in the vehicle.

"Sit down." He gestured toward the edge of the cargo area.

Lauren cringed. The last thing she was up for was a chat. Especially when this thing between them had escalated into something she didn't understand. Something she needed to put a stop to.

"I'm beat," she said, wondering if he heard the nervous trill in her voice. "I think I'd better head on into the house for a shower and a bite to eat."

"That sounds like heaven." He pushed firmly against her shoulder until she was sitting after all. "As long as you have more than a bite to eat."

He tugged the backpack from her aching shoulders, leaving them feeling unbelievably light, and replaced it with his hands. As his fingers kneaded her tight muscles, a moan of pleasure escaped her. The sound was startling, reminding her yet again of how he had elicited the same response from her a few hours earlier. She was sure he felt her stiffen beneath his hands.

"Listen," he said, "you don't have to go through this again tomorrow, you know."

Good, she thought. Trying to ignore her attraction for him was sheer torture.

"Although I must admit," he continued, "that I couldn't have accomplished half of what I did without you."

She realized he hadn't been referring to her dilemma at all. But he was offering her a way out. For a moment she said nothing, as the urge to run from her feelings for him battled with her need to be responsible, to do the right thing.

"No, I'll meet you again tomorrow," she said finally. She stood, surprised that her legs held her. "What time?"

"Same as today," he answered, handing her the backpack.

"Well . . . I waited on you for a while." She rubbed her wrist. "My watch is broken, so I don't know what time we started."

A dark look crossed his face. "I got here at six-thirty. What time did you start waiting?"

She chewed the inside of her cheek, wondering why she felt she'd done something wrong. "I was ready at five."

"A.M.? Five o'clock A.M.?" He threw his hands in the air and turned away from her. "Damn," he muttered. When he turned back toward her, his expression was determined. "Tomorrow I go it alone."

Lauren decided she'd better change her approach. "How about we make it seven and you bring breakfast?"

He hesitated, looking into her eyes. "Go," he said finally, pointing toward the house. "Eat—shower—sleep, and I'll see you in the morning."

She pushed down an illogical feeling of satisfaction. He seemed concerned about her. She let her mind drift, thinking how wonderful it would be to have someone watch out for her, see to her needs for a change. She lifted her hand in a silent good-bye as his Jeep disappeared around the corner of the driveway.

A heavy panting and the sound of claws against concrete were all she heard before Lucky slammed into the backs of her knees. Miraculously she managed to stay on her feet, too thankful for the interruption to be angry at the pup. She squatted down to tousle the long golden fur on his back.

"Hey, buddy, where were you off to?" He nestled his muzzle against her armpit, seemingly oblivious to the fact that she desperately needed a shower.

She lifted his foxlike chin to look him in the eyes. "Any man or beast willing to overlook the way I smell right now is after my own heart." She hoisted the backpack over one arm. "You just won yourself a place at the supper table, you lucky dog. Come on."

Stripping off her filthy clothes and underthings in the kitchen, she dumped them directly into the washer and liberally poured in detergent. Once the clothes were agitating, she grabbed her short robe from a peg near the laundry nook and snuggled into it. It had been expensive and rather ornate when she first purchased it, but now the soft cotton had been washed to an unrecognizable shade of blue. She decided she liked it better that way.

She padded barefoot to the refrigerator, with Lucky trailing her so closely, she could feel his hot breath on her legs. He was obviously taking his new and very temporary role as a house dog seriously.

Lauren was surprised to see a note taped to her freezer door. She pulled it off, immediately recognizing Cassie's oversize handwriting, and read: Came by to share some of the spoils of civilization with you but you weren't here. Will call tomorrow. P.S.—Don't eat the Chinese food in the refrigerator. You don't deserve it for standing me up.

Chinese food in the refrigerator! Lauren felt like she'd won the lottery. She was too tired to stand, much less fix something to eat. And she was starved. She pulled open the refrigerator door to find a large paper container, the red dragon printed on its side partially covered by a second note from Cassie.

She took the food from the shelf and pulled off the note. The corners of her mouth twitched at her younger sister's off-brand sense of humor as she read: Took a message from someone who heard about the stable—his name and number are above the phone. P.S. I told you not to eat the Chinese food. Love ya, Cassie.

Lauren gave an anxious Lucky her cold egg roll, and in a microwave minute, had devoured a full plate of Mongolian beef. As soon as she was done, she felt like a deflated tire. Every mile she had walked came back to haunt her, tugging her fatigued muscles into knotted balls.

By the time she'd cleaned up, it was all she could do to run a tub full of steaming water and disappear into its enveloping warmth. Within minutes, her muscles had relaxed. Unfortunately, so had her eyelids. She did a makeshift job of washing her hair in the tub and scrubbed the grime from her body until her skin was raw.

A quick comb through her wet hair was all she bothered with before slipping on her favorite silk gown. She smiled. It never failed to make her feel feminine again, even on days when she had to go toe-to-toe with every man she worked with. She brushed her teeth, reset the alarm clock, and made her way to bed, oblivious to the fact that it was barely eight o'clock.

She had already slid beneath the covers when she realized she hadn't put Lucky out. The gangly puppy trotted over to her bed, lifting one paw to rest on the mattress.

"Okay, you, maybe one night won't hurt," she said.

Lucky gave a small yip and placed his other paw on the bed, a mischievous glimmer in his eyes.

"No way, kiddo. I know you're relatively clean, but relatively doesn't cut it when we're talking about my bed." She glanced at her white comforter and gave Lucky a stern look. "Stay," she commanded.

The last thing she remembered was burying her face in her pillow and thinking what wonderful inventions beds were.

By seven o'clock the next morning, Lauren had managed to dress, put on a pot of coffee, and vacuum dog hair from her comforter. And after she gave Lucky a lengthy scolding, the puppy was more than happy to give up his house-dog status for an early-morning squirrel chase.

Lauren poured herself a cup of coffee and watched the energetic young dog out the window. "Some days I wish I had a dog's life," she muttered as she watched him dart into the woods after another squirrel. She added a lump of sugar to her coffee mug and stirred. "Definitely less stress."

And stress was what she felt the minute she heard Jesse's Jeep in the driveway. She stepped away from the window, not wanting him to think she'd been watching for his arrival, and busied herself refilling a napkin holder, waiting for the doorbell to ring.

Instead she heard the crumpling of a paper sack, and turned to find Jesse standing behind her in the kitchen. He wore a faded pair of blue jeans and a simple white T-shirt that darkened his tan and black hair. Tight and well-worn, the T-shirt clung to the contours of his chest like a second skin. She found herself straining to see each ripple of muscle beneath it.

He hadn't bothered to pull his hair back into its usual ponytail, and instead the dark layers fell about his face and skimmed the collar of his T-shirt in perfect disarray. Perfect because that was Jesse. He was more intelligent than any of the pompous stuffed shirts she had worked with, yet he didn't seek anyone else's approval. And that gave him a sort of freedom. She hadn't realized it until now, but it was the same sort of freedom she'd been searching for when she'd decided to open the stable.

His gaze skimmed her from head to toe, and she suddenly wished she'd worn something more attractive than blue jeans and a sleeveless chambray shirt.

"Good morning." His deep voice echoed through the big kitchen. Or maybe it was because she was standing there slack-jawed, saying nothing, that his voice seemed to echo.

"Good morning," she managed, continuing to stuff napkins into the holder.

"I see you decided to forgo the long-sleeved shirt today."

He hadn't taken his eyes off her yet, a fact that both unnerved her and made her curiously happy. "I decided to compromise because of the heat. And you?" She nodded toward his worn-thin blue jeans.

He set the white-and-orange paper sack on the table and spread his arms wide. "I compromised too."

Oh, if he only knew what that simple gesture had done to the muscles beneath his shirt—and her already jangled nerves. Lauren fumbled for an empty coffee cup and filled it without asking. She welcomed the fragrant steam that drifted up from the coffee carafe and breathed deeply, trying to center her thoughts on the day ahead instead of on the gorgeous male who was currently settling himself at her kitchen table.

She placed the cup of coffee in front of him. "Next time will you compromise a little more and ring the bell?"

"Oh, sorry." He winked at her. "I assumed you unlocked it for me." His eyebrows formed a menacing line, transforming his chocolate-warm eyes into dark pits. "You do lock it at night, don't you?"

There it was again, that dangerous heat that spread through her every time he seemed concerned. What had happened to the Lauren who relished her new independence, the one who wouldn't accept help from a man if her life depended on it? After all, every time she had, there had been strings attached. Strings that had threatened to paralyze her, pull her down.

"Of course I lock it at night." She retrieved silverware, napkins, and two plates from the cabinet before she returned to sit next to Jesse. "I unlocked the door this morning to let Lucky out."

Jesse rubbed his hand across his chin as if in thought. "I didn't think you kept him indoors."

Lauren sighed, thinking that none of this was really his business. She avoided his eyes by sorting their silverware. "Actually I don't. He just seemed to want to stay so badly last night that I let him spend the night with me."

Jesse gave her a sideways glance. "Lucky, huh?"

She felt her face go beet-red, and stared at the butter knife she held, suddenly wanting to do him bodily harm. One thing she had respected about Jesse was his straightforward nature. She hadn't thought suggestive remarks were his style.

Now she was angry at him for disappointing her, for making her feel so ill at ease.

She met his eyes, fighting the drowning feeling that always overtook her when she looked into their seemingly bottomless depths. "I don't consider comments like that flirtatious. I consider them childish."

He stared at her a moment, then smiled, an engaging dimple appearing on one cheek. When she didn't respond, he tugged the knife from her hand. "I guess I'd better take this before I get speared."

He went about pulling plastic containers from the sack as if she'd said nothing out of the ordinary. Opening one container, he plucked out a plump biscuit and quickly split it with the knife before sliding it onto her plate. He opened a second container and leaned near her to pour a river of sausage gravy over the steaming biscuit.

Jesse caught one drip of the gravy with his finger and finished it with his tongue. He met her eyes, an amused grin on his face.

"For the record," he said, "I was only going to ask you why you named him Lucky."

Lauren watched Jesse as he spread out the tarp and began to unload the canvas bag for the second time that day. If he shared any of the awkwardness she felt because of her unfair remarks that morning, it didn't show. On the contrary, he'd been wearing a sly grin all day. She bit the inside of her lip as she watched him, thinking she probably had the starring role in his private joke.

As she took a swig of lukewarm water from her thermos, she looked with envy at Jesse's icy water jug. True, she'd started out with ice water, but after six hours in the sun, it was now the temperature of a summer mud puddle. Jesse, on the other hand, had started out with a milk jug of frozen water which continually melted, providing him with something cool to drink all day.

Yesterday had been hot, but today was blanketed with humidity as well. The air seemed to linger in her lungs as she breathed, and she and Jesse couldn't go for more than thirty minutes or so without stopping and replenishing lost fluids, which had slowed things down considerably. As of yet, they had only completed one test hole, and their energy as well as their daylight was becoming limited.

Still, she was looking forward to helping Jesse with this test dig. She had taken him to a small rise that bordered the creek bank, recalling that as kids she and Cassie had collected handfuls of arrowheads there after a bad spring flood.

So far, Jesse had been rather closemouthed about the results of the first two test holes. He'd filled up a dozen or so zip-top bags with what looked like dirt to her, and explained that they would have to be examined at the university before he knew exactly what they had. She was disappointed that the only artifact they had found so far was merely a chipped arrowhead.

Something would turn up. It had to. She looked at the elevated area that sloped toward the creek bank. She had a feeling that if anything did turn up, it would be here.

She joined Jesse on the tarp, and knelt down to slip off her backpack.

"Lauren . . ."

The sound of his voice caught her off guard. As she looked up, a horsefly landed on her nose and she swatted frantically at it, pulling down half of her braid and practically coating her face with dirt from her fingers before the fly gave up and flew away.

Jesse's soft laugh made her look up again. "I see you don't feel as charitable toward horseflies as you do barn mice."

"No, I don't," she said, glancing around her to make sure the fly had gone. She tried to tuck the loose strands of hair back into what was left of her braid, but gave up, deciding she was only calling attention to her unkempt appearance.

She felt Jesse's gaze still on her and looked back at him, then grew even more embarrassed by the grim look on his face. She must look like something that crawled out from under a rock, she thought.

"Since we're not far from the house," he said, "would you mind getting my sling blade from the Jeep?" He gestured toward the creek. "I want to dig here at the edge of the rise, and the underbrush is thicker than I thought."

She stood up and stretched her aching shoulders. "Sure. No problem."

The short hike home would break up the monotony and give her an opportunity to center her thoughts on the task at hand, instead of concentrating on such things as the way Jesse's damp T-shirt clung to his shoulders and chest. Besides, she could use the bathroom and freshen up a little.

Jesse opened an oversize zip-top bag and pulled out graph paper and a clipboard. "I'll be making some records and taking pictures for a while, so take your time." He squinted, looking up at her. "Why don't you go inside your house and get out of the heat? You look like you could use a break."

Lauren wanted to disappear on the spot, wondering just how bad she did look. "No, that's okay. Do I need your keys to the Jeep?"

He stood, squeezing his hand into the front pocket of his jeans. They were damp and clinging with perspiration, and she watched his thigh muscles strain against the fabric as he maneuvered the keys from his pocket. The heat from the sun seemed to radiate and swirl about her, burning her cheeks and sending droplets of sweat raining between her breasts. He tossed her the keys, breaking the spell.

"The sling blade is the one with a long, thick handle and a curved blade that—"

She turned her back to him and began to walk away, taking in deep gulps of air. "I know what a sling blade is," she called over her shoulder.

She literally stomped her way to the Jeep. As if she didn't know what a sling blade was! When she'd first moved there, the grounds had been so overgrown, she'd had to use the sling blade to clear a path to the barn.

Her eyes stung as she recalled how discouraged she'd been as she'd pulled the vines from the rusted blades of her grandfather's bush hog. The tractor had been idle so long that the underbrush had completely surrounded it. She glanced around her, allowing herself to feel a surge of hard-won pride at how far she'd come.

She paused to trace a raised white scar on one knuckle, a war wound from that first day, before pushing the key in the lock of the hatchback and releasing it. When she peered into the cargo area, she couldn't help but laugh. That was, no doubt, the littlest sling blade she had ever seen. Well, today she would introduce Jesse McCain to a real scythe.

She marched back toward the barn, feeling vindicated already. Plucking her own sling blade from just inside the door, she hoisted the heavy tool over one shoulder and headed back to the test site. Before long, though, she began to wish she'd taken time to at least splash some cool water on her face. A few more minutes, and she felt fat droplets of sweat traveling along her hairline, making her want to slap at imaginary flies.

By the time she reached the tarp, she was so hot and out of breath that she could barely balance the sling blade on her shoulder any longer. She let it drop a little harder than she'd intended and winced as she saw the blade cut through the tarp and impale the earth underneath.

She had rehearsed what she was going to say. What was it again? She extended the tool toward him. His image was unclear because of the droplets of perspiration that kept spilling into her eyes, but she thought she saw him glance at his watch. "I figured you might want to use my sling blade. It's bigger."

He took the heavy tool from her, and she was immediately relieved. Now she needed some water. If she didn't get some soon, her knees were going to buckle. Without consciously planning it, she turned and headed toward the creek.

"Lauren, where are you going?" Jesse called after her.

She concentrated on making her voice sound as normal and cheerful as possible. "I'm just going to take a little break. I'll be right back to help you."

Plowing her way through the dense tangle of honeysuckle, she tried to avoid the clumps of low-growing poison oak, but her feet didn't seem to land where she aimed them. Eventually she reached the creek bank. The canopy of leaves overhead gave her some respite from the heat, and her head began to clear.

In front of her the creek rolled lazily by, its crystal clear water inviting her to quench her thirst. But her heart sank when she eyed the steep bank. That would take some careful maneuvering.

She made her way to a fallen oak tree and used it as a seat while she removed her socks and shoes. She tried to roll up her jeans, but the tight cuff only gave a couple of inches before it bound against her ankle. Sighing, she strained to see Jesse over the ridge and through the tangle of leaves. It was either take her jeans off, or go in with them on and spend the rest of the day wet and uncomfortable. Or she could skip the creek altogether.

Her throat was parched and aching, and bits of broken poison oak clung to her ankles. No, the jeans were coming off and if Jesse showed up, she would just send him packing. She unzipped her jeans and stepped out of them, relieved to see that her shirttail covered her bottom. She tossed her jeans over the fallen tree and, clinging to a willow tree that leaned over the creek, lowered herself down the steep bank.

Lauren felt positively giddy as she stepped into the water. Balancing on one flat moss-covered rock, she wiggled her toes against the spongy surface before stepping off and into the knee-deep water. A surge of cold vibrated through her and took her breath away. The water was just as icy as it had been when she was a kid. Cupping her hands, she scooped up water and drank the soothing liquid until she was forced to break for air.

She waded around a bit, eventually becoming used to the numbing cold, and scattering schools of small bass as she went. Finally she made her way to a spot where the smooth, flat rocks of the creek's bottom broke the surface, forming one of many miniature waterfalls. She tied her shirttail in a knot and sat down on one of the rocks, straightening her legs out in front of her and letting the water rush against her feet and through her toes.

She splashed water on her face, scrubbing away the sweat and grime as she did. Feeling more like herself than she had since Jesse first showed up a week ago, she unbraided her hair and threw her head back, letting the sunlight that filtered through the trees evaporate the drops of water that clung to her. She sighed. She'd pretend she was a kid again—just for a little while.

Somewhere on the creek bank a frog leaped in. And then another. Lauren opened her eyes to investigate.

"You know, it's hard to find good help these days." Jesse's voice was like a clap of thunder when you weren't expecting rain. Lauren jumped, pressing her palm against her chest to keep her heart from leaping out.

He was standing in the knee-deep water, toying with the end of a willow strand. He'd shed his T-shirt but still wore his jeans. Lauren swallowed hard. The force of the rushing water pulling against the denim had lowered the waistband of his jeans enough to reveal a straight, dark line of hair that disappeared from sight amidst a backdrop of fairer skin.

It registered in some remote corner of her brain that she was staring, but she was at a loss as to what to do about it. Well, at least she wouldn't allow herself to look any lower. She realized that wasn't the best of plans, as her gaze traveled upward. Smooth and tan, his upper body revealed sinewy muscles earned by hard work, not stationary gym equipment.

"You can't come in here," she said finally.

He laughed. "I'm already in here."

"I'm not dressed."

"Well, *I'm* not looking."

He waded through the water and, to her distress, sat down on a rock next to her. She was assaulted by his nearness, by the brush of his bare arm against hers, the intoxicating scent of his wet skin. She wanted to bolt from the creek. She wanted to press against his warm chest, taste his skin. She began to tremble and drew her knees up, clasping her hands across them to stop their shaking.

"That's a hell of a sling blade you have." He didn't look at her, but stared straight ahead.

"Thanks," was all she could think to say.

She glanced in his direction, but looked away again as her mind started to recall how he'd felt atop her, his weight pressing her against the ground. The trembling was now moving from her hands to the rest of her body.

"I'll bet it was heavy carrying it all the way back," Jesse commented.

His words slowly sank in. He intentionally carried such puny-looking equipment because the heavy-duty kind was too . . . well, heavy.

"Okay." She was surprised to hear that even her voice was trembling. "I get your point."

His hand settled against the back of her neck, firm and warm against her chilled skin. "You're shaking."

Yes, she thought, and if he kept touching her, she was going to shake until she fell apart. She had to put some distance between them. She clamped her jaw shut, trying to stop the shaking before she spoke again.

"I think I went from one extreme to the other," she lied. She untied her shirttail and stood, smoothing the wet material over her hips. "I'd better get out now."

"Yeah, me too." Jesse stood.

"No, you stay and cool off. You're already wet. You might as well take advantage of it."

As she waded back to the willow tree, she glanced over her shoulder at him. He must know she had to scramble back up the steep bank on all fours, but continued to watch anyway. Well, she wasn't prepared to lose that much modesty in one day. Instead, she waded up the creek. There was a low spot in the bank several yards away. She would use it instead.

One run-in with a water moccasin as a child had taught her to keep a close eye on the creek bank, which was what she was doing when a strange-looking rock caught her attention.

It was rounded and smooth, an unusual solid color despite the spattering of moss that clung to it. As she leaned over and touched it, it broke away from the creek bank and fell into her hands. She turned the rock over, realizing that it wasn't a rock at all, but a piece of pottery. She bent closer, scraping her index finger against the soft soil that had held it in place.

As she probed harder, her fingernail tapped against something solid.

"What is it?" Jesse called from behind her.

Her curiosity was up, and Lauren almost resented the interruption. "I don't know," she called back.

She plucked a twig from the bank and continued to probe at the object until it broke away from the mud. She laid it in her palm and began to scrape away the soil. It looked like a coin of some sort. She dipped it in the water to wash away the clinging dirt.

She could hear Jesse splashing through the water behind her, and as she straightened she immediately sensed his nearness. His body radiated heat against the back of her arm as he leaned to look over her shoulder.

"Give it to me." He sounded tense, like a stranger.

She dropped it into his palm. "It's a coin. It has some type of writing on it. Can you make it out?"

He held it close to his face, his voice barely a whisper. "Carlos Et Iohana Reges . . ."

"What?"

"Carlos and Johanna Rule," he answered, his voice oddly distant. "It's a sixteenth-century Spanish coin."

A dark expression marred his face, and he looked sharply back at the creek bank.

"But then you knew that, didn't you?" he said.

SIX

"What surprises me is that she was able to get it so fast," Ken said, one side of his round face illuminated by the examination light as he inspected the coin.

Jesse ran his hand across his chin, his fingers rasping over the stubble there. He'd been too distracted that morning to do anything but drive straight to the university.

"She's not dumb by any means," he said to Ken. "When we got back to her place yesterday, I noticed a stack of books on artifacts and local history stashed in a corner of her kitchen." He hit the thick black top of the lab table with his fist. "Damn, but I should have seen it coming."

"You know there's something you're not considering here, my friend." Ken switched off the examination light.

"What's that?"

"Maybe she didn't plant it."

Jesse couldn't help but laugh, and the bitterness in that laugh echoed across the lab's tile floor. Oh, he'd entertained the idea that the artifact was genuine. For about a second. What had wrenched his gut, though, was Lauren's choice. She had no doubt visited the newspaper archives, read the accounts of the failed Coosa excavation, and picked an artifact that she thought would push his buttons.

And it would have, if he hadn't seen through her ruse. An artifact like the coin would have been a dream come true at the Coosa site. It would have proven that the Coosa chiefdom had finally been located, and that the early Spanish explorers had occupied it. More importantly, it would have meant that he and Luke were right. Instead, all they had discovered were layers of stone and brown clay. And their own humility.

The real irony of the whole thing was how he'd agonized over keeping the truth from Lauren, worrying about how she'd react when he finally told her.

Ken laid the coin on a piece of black felt and took several pictures of it before turning it over and repeating the process.

"Hey," Jesse said as Ken finished. "Keep those to yourself once they're developed, will you?" He met Ken's puzzled look. "I don't want to have to explain."

Ken nodded. "Well, what about it?"

"What about what?"

The lab table squeaked loudly as Ken leaned against it. "What if the coin's for real? I don't have to tell you what it would mean if the area was part of early Spanish exploration."

Jesse raised an eyebrow and grunted. His interest in tracing the Soto and Luna expeditions had died along with his theory about the Coosa chiefdom. "The only thing this artifact tells me is that Lauren Adams has gotten to know her local antique coin dealer."

Ken laughed, using his best cartoon laugh, which was guaranteed to lighten up any conversation. "Maybe. But if not, it could be major, major stuff, Professor McCain."

"Well, buying in to this hoax would end any chance of a teaching career for me once and for all."

"And if it's not a hoax, you could actually lease your apartment for longer than six months at a time." Ken playfully tugged Jesse's ponytail. "You might have to lose this, but the classroom is a helluva lot cooler in the summer. Why not look into it?"

Jesse swatted Ken's hand away, a pensive expression replacing his smile. "For starters, the Soto expedition didn't come within fifty miles of the Adams property, and nothing—I repeat, nothing—else of Spanish origin has ever been found there."

"Well, it's never been excavated before. Besides, unless I miss my mark, it couldn't have come from the Hernando de Soto expedition. The coin isn't that old."

Jesse suppressed a surge of professional curiosity. "The coin was planted. It doesn't make any difference."

Ignoring Jesse's comment, Ken switched the light back on and motioned for Jesse to join him. "Look beside the Spanish crest. See the letter *L*?"

Jesse nodded.

"That's the mark of the assayer of the Mexico City mint. *L* would be for Luis Rodriguez. I checked. He didn't become the assayer until 1554. Soto's expedition was almost twenty years earlier."

The dates swam in Jesse's head. "That would mean

the coin was probably brought by the Tristan de Luna expedition."

Ken nodded. "Which would be more evidence that the Coosa chiefdom was where you and Luke theorized. If you were right about Coosa—"

"I wasn't right about Coosa." Jesse scowled at Ken. "We researched until we were blue in the face; we plotted and planned; we convinced the Early Exploration Commission to fund the dig. And oh—" He threw back his head and laughed. "I invited the damned media."

"Am I interrupting?" Luke Ebsin's familiar voice penetrated the room with soft authority.

Damn, Jesse thought. How much had he heard? His own fascination with early exploration hadn't been born in a vacuum. It had been Luke's determination to trace the paths of the Spanish explorers, to locate the Native American chiefdoms they inhabited, that had fueled Jesse's enthusiasm as an undergraduate. Somehow over the years Luke Ebsin had become the father, and Jesse the son eager to follow in his footsteps.

If Luke now thought there was a trace of evidence . . . Jesse felt sick. He couldn't watch him endure more humiliation. "How much did you hear?"

Luke Ebsin, long accustomed to Jesse's bluntness, eased his tall, slender frame onto a lab stool with the grace of someone half his age. He hesitated a moment, then looked at Jesse. "I didn't know we had secrets."

Jesse found he had to look away from the crystal blue eyes of his mentor, eyes that always seemed to see more than Jesse wanted him to. "No secrets. Just cataloging some artifacts from the highway department's salvage excavation."

"Oh." The professor glanced at Ken. "Anything of interest?"

Ken slid the coin, which he had hidden in the square of black felt, across the table. Jesse took it and nonchalantly placed it back in his zippered attaché case.

Anything of interest? He recalled Lauren lounging half-naked in the creek, and felt his face flush with anger. How stupid he had been. The setup couldn't be more obvious to him now, but at the time . . .

He cleared his throat. "No, nothing worthwhile."

At the time all he had seen was Lauren Adams.

Lauren sat cross-legged in the rocking chair that occupied a corner of her kitchen, a huge library book digging into her bare legs.

She rubbed her temples as she lost her concentration again. What had Jesse meant when he said she knew the coin was of Spanish origin? When she'd asked, he'd only shaken his head and gone about the business of recording the find. She tried to convince herself that she'd only imagined the angry tone in his voice, but the nagging feeling wouldn't go away.

She thumped her index finger against the open page. "This one looks just like the one I found, except someone has drilled a hole in it."

Cassie continued to paw through the contents of the refrigerator, nothing but her blue-jean-clad derriere visible from where Lauren sat.

"Are you listening to me?" Lauren asked.

"Yes, I am, but I could concentrate better if you had something to eat around here. Don't you know it's lunchtime?"

"Honestly, you act like you couldn't care less," Lauren said, more than a little irritated with her sister. Cassie's indifference when she'd told her about the coin had been disappointing.

Still, Lauren was trying not to overreact. She hadn't realized just how pent-up her emotions had been until she'd held the artifact in her hands—and realized she might have found her ticket out of this mess.

Her sister turned to face her. "Lauren, you know better than that. It's just that I don't want you to get your hopes up. It could be worthless for all you know."

Well, worthless was one thing she knew it wasn't. She'd gone back to the local library that morning and had tried to find the coin in one of the many volumes of books on antique coins. She hadn't found it. None of the volumes had even listed coins that old.

The closest she'd come to spotting a similar coin had been in a book on Alabama archaeology, the book that was now spread open in her lap. She traced the uneven edges of the coin in the photo, squinting in an attempt to read the inscription, but she couldn't make out the letters in the yellowed black-and-white picture.

"Listen to this, Cassie. 'Other items found at the site were three shell-tempered vessels with feature ten and a copper gorget—' "

"Condense, condense!" Cassie wailed, her voice echoing in the near-empty pantry that she was searching.

Lauren sighed and finished reading the paragraph to herself. "Well, basically it says the coin was found in a Native American burial site in south Alabama." She ran her finger along the lines of text as she scanned the next page. "Judging from some of the other European items there, they believe the site was a chiefdom occupied by the Spanish during their exploration of the Southeast."

Cassie looked up from her examination of a cupboard. "But would that make it important enough to stop the highway project? I mean, assuming that you've got the same sort of rest stop here?"

Lauren rolled her eyes. Leave it to Cassie to sum things up like that. "According to this, it might." She marked the page with a paper clip, intending to read it more carefully later. "It might mean that they could pinpoint the exact route the explorers took. From what little I've read so far, that seems to be a hot debate topic."

Cassie crossed the kitchen, snatched up a pad and pencil from Lauren's stack of research materials, went to the phone, and punched in a phone number with the eraser end of the pencil.

"Who are you calling?" Lauren wondered if she had spurred Cassie into action with her brief but informative history lesson. From the determined look on her face, Cassie could be calling the governor.

"Pizza Express."

Lauren shook her head in disbelief. "They won't deliver way out here, dummy. They'd never find their way."

"They're about to learn. Besides, if Hans is on duty, he'll make an exception."

"Hans?"

"His family is from Germany. He's working his way through law school." Cassie turned her attention back to the phone. "Yes, I'll hold." She looked at Lauren and winked. "Gorgeous blue eyes and great buns."

Before Lauren could form a polite response, Lucky began barking outside. It was his serious bark, the one reserved for strangers and wild animals that ventured too close. Lauren looked at her watch, and her stomach gave a nervous roll. Freeway interchange or not, she had to get on with the business at hand. If luck was with her, there was a man pulling into her driveway whose horse would become her first boarder.

When she'd dialed the telephone number Cassie had taken down for her, she had expected only to pass along some general information about the stable and maybe a tentative opening date. Instead she'd learned that Ted Clarke wanted to lease a stall immediately, and he seemed unconcerned that the grounds weren't ready and that he would likely have the only horse stabled there for some time. In fact, he'd sounded pleased.

Lauren opened her front door to find Ted Clarke kneeling down next to his car, nothing but a headful of wavy brown hair showing as he gave Lucky an affectionate scratch behind the ears.

At least she assumed the man was her potential customer. He looked younger than she'd expected, and the expensive-looking blue Cadillac behind him was a surprise as well. Somehow, the heavy Southern accent she'd heard over the phone had conjured images of a pickup truck and a baseball cap.

He looked up and smiled as she approached, and she was immediately struck by how handsome he was. Rather short but athletically built, his light blue eyes radiated a genuine warmth.

He brushed off his hand on his crisply pressed khaki shorts before extending it toward her. "You must be Lauren Adams."

She shook his hand, surprised to find it firm and

work roughened, though not as much as Jesse's. "Yes. And you must be Mr. Clarke."

"Ted, please."

She smiled, thinking he seemed nice, the sort of customer she had hoped to attract. "Well, Ted, I'm sorry about my ferocious watchdog."

He gave her an incredulous look and ruffled the fur on the back of Lucky's neck. "I hate to tell you this, but he could take aggression lessons from my daughter's cat."

Lauren laughed. "You mentioned over the phone that the horse you want to board is your daughter's."

"Yes, well . . . He will be." Ted shoved his hands into the pockets of his shorts. "What I mean is, I've just bought him. He's going to be a surprise for her tenth birthday."

"What a wonderful gift." Lauren thought he seemed a little unsure of himself, but decided not to ask any questions. "Follow me and I'll show you the barn."

She flipped on the lights as they entered. Ted Clarke's expression immediately went from cheerful to analytical, and Lauren was glad she'd gotten up early that morning to tidy the inside of the barn. No doubt there was a shrewd businessman behind Ted's friendly face.

That thought brought a defensive edge to her voice as she said, "As I told you over the phone, I hadn't planned to take on any boarders until all the renovations were complete."

When he turned to her again, he was smiling. "I was just thinking how perfect this is going to be." He walked over to her and rested one hand on her shoulder.

"You're actually not much taller than my daughter," he said casually.

Lauren swallowed hard, trying to act casual herself. Nothing about this man would make her think he wasn't a decent guy, but she was becoming uncomfortable with his nearness.

"Do you mind if I ask you something personal?" he went on. Before she could answer, he continued, "How much do you weigh?"

Part of her wanted to remove his hand from her shoulder, but her instincts told her there was a good reason for his strange behavior. "Why do you ask?" she finally responded.

"That's what I was wondering myself." Jesse's voice thundered across the barn.

Lauren spun around, feeling as if she'd been caught doing something illicit. Jesse stood in the doorway of the barn, silhouetted by the glare of the overcast day behind him, his hands planted on his hips. She felt Ted's hand slip from her shoulder.

"Jesse."

He strode toward her, stopping when he was an inch away. He placed his arm around her shoulders and firmly pulled her back a step from Ted.

"You must be Lauren's husband." Ted's expression was more reserved as he extended his hand toward Jesse.

Jesse grasped his hand, not correcting the mistake.

"I'm Ted Clarke," he continued. "I'll be boarding my horse here at Lauren's stable." He looked pointedly at Lauren. "That is, if the offer still stands."

"Of course," Lauren said, her voice shaky.

Jesse released Ted's hand, and Ted shoved both of his hands deep into his shorts pockets. "I was about to ask

Lauren if she'd be willing to work with my daughter's horse. He's a pony cross, which makes him a little too stubborn for a kid—and too small for most trainers to work with. But I think Lauren would be the perfect size."

Lauren was flattered, not to mention relieved. "Normally I'd say yes, Mr. Clarke," she answered, "but with all the work still left to do on the barn, I'm afraid I'll have to say no. I simply don't have the time."

Jesse locked his knees and hooked his thumb through the front belt loop of his jeans. "Maybe that's something your wife could help you with?"

Ted looked suddenly tired as he rocked back on his heels, seeming to study the laces of his expensive docker shoes. "I'd make it financially worth your while," he said, meeting Lauren's eyes again and ignoring Jesse's comment.

"I really do appreciate your offer, but to be honest with you I don't have any formal training to share with your daughter. As I told you on the phone, the stable will just be a place where families board their horses for recreation, not a show barn."

"Are you capable of seeing that he's safe for her to ride?"

"Yes, I grew up riding and working with horses, but—"

"That's all I want for Alyssa." Ted continued to stare at her, as if waiting to hear a reason he'd accept.

Lauren squirmed under his scrutiny. "I would be eager to work with Alyssa's horse, if I had the time, but . . ." She shrugged helplessly.

"I understand," Ted said.

Lauren mentally prepared herself for him to change

his mind about boarding with her altogether, but she wasn't ready to lose the badly needed income without a fight. "I can guarantee you the horse will be fed only top quality hay and feed, and that his stall will be cleaned daily."

"I'm not looking for anything fancy. I just need to make sure the horse is safe enough for my daughter to ride."

"I'm not sure that's Lauren's problem, Mr. Clarke," Jesse interrupted. "It sounds as if that's something you and your wife should have considered before you bought the horse."

Lauren was about to give Jesse a piece of her mind for intruding on her business, when Ted spoke up. "My *wife* was killed in a car accident, Mr. Adams."

"It's McCain," Jesse said, his voice soft, the look in his eyes regretful.

Ted brushed past Jesse and Lauren and headed toward the barn door. He stopped midway and turned to face Jesse.

"The same accident, *Mr. McCain*, that left my daughter in a coma for a month." He ground the wood shavings that covered the barn floor beneath his shoe as if he were working to control his temper. When he looked at Lauren again, his face was expressionless, but his eyes appealed to her for help. "It's been a year now, and the doctor says riding will be good therapy for Alyssa. But I know next to nothing about horses."

Lauren thought about the seemingly endless summer days that she and Cassie had spent at the farm riding. She couldn't imagine what hell Ted's daughter had suffered, but she didn't have to be a professional to understand that the little girl needed help. Lauren sighed.

There wasn't a better place in the world to lose yourself in the joy of living than astride a horse.

When she opened her mouth to tell him she'd find the time to work with the horse, he threw his hand up, as if to stop her.

"Go ahead and reserve a stall for the horse, Lauren, and think about my offer. I'll be in touch."

She followed Ted out of the barn, staring after his car until the smooth hum of the Cadillac faded into the distance. Then she turned to Jesse, but couldn't find the words to tell him just what she thought of him at that moment. Instead, she stormed toward the house, feeling her pulse pounding against her temples, the first sign that she was getting a stress headache.

And she hadn't had a stress headache since she'd left her old job, or more specifically, the source of stress there—men.

Well, this was one man who was about to learn his lesson when it came to control. This was her life and her business, and just because she was forced to accept his help at the moment didn't give him license to put his nose in where it didn't belong.

And it certainly didn't belong in Ted Clarke's personal life. The poor man had enough to deal with. It was a wonder he hadn't left earlier.

She almost knocked Cassie over as she burst through the front door. "Sorry," she barked.

"Whoa, Sis," Cassie said as she dodged to one side of the foyer. "What's eating you?"

"Men!" Lauren yelled as she stomped toward the kitchen.

Cassie did her best Mae West voice as she followed behind her. "Don't you wish?"

"That's not funny." Lauren jerked the portable phone from its cradle and began to search through the papers on the kitchen table.

"What are you looking for?" Cassie asked.

"Mr. Harbison's number. Got it," she said as she tapped the back of her spiral notebook. "I'm about to exorcise one Jesse McCain from my life. Mr. Harbison should have the coin by now, and I don't see why Jesse should be hanging around for much longer."

"Exorcisms are for demons, big sister." Cassie cleared her throat. "Although from what I've seen of his body, he is devilishly—"

"Stop it," Lauren interrupted. She punched the rubber buttons on the phone with more force than was necessary, then waited for the call to go through. "Damn, it's busy."

Cassie draped her arm around Lauren's shoulders. "Come on, let's take a walk. You can tell me what he's done that you're overreacting to, and then you can try Harbison's office again."

"I am *not* overreacting!" Sometimes she wondered whose side Cassie was on, anyway. But Lauren had to admit that the walk sounded like a good idea. She didn't need to talk with the president of the highway commission when she was in such a temper.

By the time they reached the paddock next to the barn, Lauren had given her sister a blow-by-blow account of the incident with Ted, and she felt just as indignant about it as she had before. When she looked at Cassie, she was certain her sister would apologize for accusing her of overreacting.

And she needed Cassie to be on her side for once, because she was about to ask her for a favor.

"So, Bones was jealous, huh?" Cassie had a definite smirk on her face.

Lauren sighed. Leave it to Cassie's brain to work on that frequency. Well, she had to admit that the same thought had crossed her mind, but she was certain Jesse was more interested in his ego than in her.

Lauren took a calming breath, determined not to let Cassie get to her. "I don't know what he was other than rude." She tapped the antenna of the phone against the paddock fence. "I felt so sorry for Ted, though, I could have cried."

"Yeah, no kidding. That's a tough break," Cassie said, tucking a short lock of blond hair behind her ear.

"Listen, how would you feel about helping out?" Lauren looked into her sister's eyes as she asked the question, and immediately saw the skepticism.

"I don't like the sound of that," Cassie said. "Just what did you have in mind?"

"I told you that Ted needs someone to work with his daughter's horse."

Cassie nodded.

"Even though I told him I'd consider it, there's just no way I can find the time."

Cassie began to shake her head. "No, no, and no."

Lauren rushed on. "You've always been a great rider, Sis, and I'll be you haven't lost your touch. Have a heart. He needs you."

"In case you've forgotten, I already have a job ped-dling . . . I mean selling real estate. You know how busy I stay."

Lauren tried not to laugh. Her sister worked smart, not hard. Well, so much for the sympathetic approach, she thought. Time to try something else. "He's your type," she said with a wink.

Cassie placed her hands on her hips. "And just what is my type according to the all-knowing, all-seeing Lauren Elizabeth Adams?"

"Good-looking," Lauren replied.

Cassie sniffed and looked away. "Tempting, but tragic men are not my forte."

"What about little girls who have been sick and need a friend?"

"Oh good grief." Cassie rolled her eyes heavenward. "Lay it on, will you?"

"Think about it," Lauren called as Cassie started to walk toward the house.

Her sister waved a hand behind her back without turning. "Yeah, yeah, I'll think about it." Then she turned and pointed a finger at Lauren, a serious expression on her face. "And you—answer the phone if it rings. Hans might need directions."

Jesse wiped the sweat from his chest with his T-shirt, then dropped the shirt onto the tarp. He'd tried to take his mind off what had happened at the barn by working at breakneck speed, moving fallen trees and clearing the heavy underbrush from the excavation site, but it hadn't helped. He knew Lauren thought he was the most heartless oaf alive. He certainly felt that way.

It had done something to him, something nameless and gut-wrenching, to see Ted Clarke touching Lauren. He'd wanted to punch the man in the face right where he stood. Jesse pulled loose the rubber band that bound his hair, and ran his fingers through the sweat-dampened strands. Hell, punching him would have been kinder than what he'd done.

It was just that he'd driven there from the university in such a temper that he'd been ready for any sort of release. And Ted Clarke had been available. Available and touching Lauren. As hard as it was to swallow, he had to admit he'd felt betrayed.

Even though it wasn't entirely logical, he felt Lauren had already betrayed him once by planting the coin. On a more rational level, he knew she was doing what she felt she had to do to save her home, but it sure felt personal. It was more than the bond between himself and Luke Ebsin. His career had been the only steadfast thing in his life. It was all he had, all he was.

Thunder rolled in the distance, and Jesse looked up. The wind was stirring, bringing a cooler breeze and a clinging dampness that carried the unmistakable scent of rain. He let the breeze play against his face, trying to release the image of Ted Clarke, and the pain that had dulled the man's eyes.

Damn, he wished he'd kept his mouth shut. And Lauren—she hadn't said anything, just walked away. That was the worst of it. He knew her temper, knew she'd been dying to give him hell, but she'd been too disgusted with him even to look at him.

A bolt of lightning cracked on the south end of the valley, and the wind began to sway the tops of the pines. Jesse shut his eyes as a miniature whirlwind lifted the sandy dirt from the old logging road, dancing it along the edge of the tall weeds before heading north toward Lauren's house.

"Lauren," he said softly, shaking his head. Lord, he'd screwed things up. He looked at the swirling dark cloud gathering on the horizon, and hoped she had stayed in her house. But knowing Lauren, she was probably disking the pasture, or unloading bales of hay, or some other monstrous task that seemed impossible for someone her size.

A fat raindrop hit the tarp, and Jesse began gathering his tools, throwing the small ones into the canvas bag alongside his field notes and half-eaten sandwich. The image of Lauren perched on the old metal tractor in the middle of the pasture had him rushing to beat the electrical storm.

He felt his concern turning to anger, but he wasn't sure why. As he'd driven from the university to Lauren's earlier, he'd been angry with Lauren, and then he certainly had been angry with Ted Clarke. Now he was more angry with himself than anyone. He had watched Lauren, seen how hard she worked, felt the hardened blisters on her hands. No matter what she'd done, she deserved a break. And from what he'd seen so far, no one was giving her one. Himself included.

All he'd done for her was lie to her, let her exhaust herself by helping him, and get in the way of her success. And he would have made love to her. If he was honest with himself, he'd admit that making love with her would have been a mistake, considering he'd never been long-term-relationship material.

Jesse thought back on the last ten years. The longest he'd stayed put had been for the Coosa dig, and even that had managed to blow up in his face. He could still see the headlines: "Professor Looks for the Past—Jeopardizes Future."

He ground the heel of his hiking boot against the tarp. No, he was probably better off doing what he'd always done, taking the assignments that no one else wanted, the ones that would take him wherever and whenever. That way, at least, he never had the chance to know what he was missing.

He left the tarp behind as he slung the canvas bag over one shoulder and headed toward Lauren's house. The woven strap rubbed against the exposed skin of his back and shoulders as he lengthened his stride.

Lauren . . . The truth was, husband-material or not, he wouldn't stop if he had it to do all over again.

"Ask Mr. Harbison to call me, then." Lauren gave the receptionist her telephone number. "And please tell him I'd like to know what the status of the project is since the artifact has been found."

The off button on the portable phone beeped as she punched it. She set the phone on the floor of the loft and looked up at the beamed ceiling, noticing absentmindedly that there was a new wasp nest she needed to knock down. She'd come here countless times growing up when she needed to think. Maybe it would help today.

A delightful, cool breeze was wafting through the loft door, a sure sign of rain. She closed her eyes, letting the breeze lift her hair. Not surprisingly, her thoughts turned immediately to Jesse. What had made him so certain that she needed or even wanted his help where Ted Clarke was concerned? She scooted to the door and slung her legs through the wide opening, dangling them over the side. A distant boom of thunder sounded, and she looked around. A storm was gathering to the south, turning the afternoon glow into an eerie shade of greenish-gray. She glanced toward her house, noticing that Jesse's Jeep was still parked next to the driveway.

She tried to tell herself that she was still too angry at him to worry whether or not he got caught by the electrical storm. A bolt of lightning cracked on the horizon, and she jumped, noticing how drastically the light had faded in just a few minutes, how the loft was suddenly filled with shadows.

She had to admit that part of her was flattered that Jesse had seemed jealous of Ted, but she knew from experience that just because a man didn't want someone else to have you didn't mean he wanted you himself. Lauren winced as she recalled the pain she'd seen on Ted Clarke's face. No wonder he'd seemed nervous about giving his daughter the horse. And to lose his wife like that . . .

Lauren shut her eyes again. She didn't want to endure the pain of that kind of loss. She pulled loose a piece of hay that had entangled itself in the ends of her hair and twirled it back and forth. She needed to find the strength to get Jesse out of her life before it was too late. There was no need to set herself up for a fall.

A rolling boom of thunder rattled the loft, and she glanced toward the old logging road. She saw nothing there but shadows and pine saplings dancing against the pull of the wind.

She hauled a bale of hay from the back of the loft over to the door and tossed an old saddle blanket over it, making an effective rest for her back. In a few minutes rain began to pelt the tin roof of the barn, drowning out the sound of the storm.

Lauren rested her face against the blanket, staring out at the old logging road. Part of her was missing when Jesse was gone. The wind howled through the tin eaves and rattled the roof. Somehow, in the shadow of the storm, she found it easy to admit what she'd feared all along. It was too late to guard her heart.

Like the inevitable thunderstorm, Lauren resigned herself to the heartache fate might bring her. Lightning cracked, and she glanced at the logging road again. Still no sign of Jesse.

She rubbed her arms, trying to quell a tremor of fear. She'd have to go to the protection of the house soon. As soon as Jesse came home to her.

SEVEN

"Lauren!"

Someone was shaking her shoulders.

"Lauren!"

Jesse's voice. Something was wrong . . . Lauren opened her eyes and bolted upright. Jesse was leaning over her, his hair wet and dripping onto his bare shoulders and chest, his eyebrows lowered in a fierce scowl. She shifted, feeling the prickle of hay against the back of her legs, and remembered that she was in the loft of the barn.

"Are you all right?" Jesse's voice thundered above the raging storm.

She looked behind her at the saddle blanket she'd been lying on and then out the loft door. How could she have fallen asleep with the storm howling only a few feet away? She'd been waiting on Jesse, thinking, then she must have dozed right off. Even as a child, falling instantly asleep had been her defense mechanism, a way of turning off her thoughts when they became too difficult to sort out. Most people couldn't sleep when they were anxious; she, on the other hand, couldn't stop herself.

"Answer me, dammit!" Jesse gave her shoulders another shake.

"I'm okay!" she yelled over the deafening sound of the rain hitting the roof of the barn. "What are you doing here?"

"Looking for you," he answered gruffly, tugging her to her feet. He pushed her toward the ladder. "Come on. The Jeep is just outside the barn door."

She climbed down the ladder, trying to shake the sleepy, groggy feeling that made her arms and legs feel like noodles. Glancing up, she saw Jesse descending after her. The muscles in his arms and shoulders were taut as he lowered himself down the ladder. Maybe the shaky feeling had more to do with waking up with Jesse hovering over her.

Finally he dropped to the floor next to her. The rain had turned his dark hair jet-black, and it fell in dripping layers about his face. His shirt was off, and the flat planes of his chest and shoulders glistened with water. He was breathing hard, as if he'd been running.

"Why were you in the loft? I thought you'd passed out or something." He was looking at her with his head cocked—as if she were out of her mind.

"I . . ." She was fully awake now, but his nearness seemed to be stealing her thoughts, muddling her ability to make sense. "I go up there sometimes when it's not too hot—to think. There was a breeze, and I just sat down for a minute. I must have fallen asleep." She realized she'd left the phone up there, but decided to get it later.

A bolt of lightning flashed so near, she could literally feel the electricity in the air.

"Dammit, Lauren, that was too close. We need to get to the house."

He wrapped his arm around her shoulders and pushed her out the barn door and into the pouring rain, eventually shoving her into the front seat of the Jeep. Before it registered that the Jeep was already running, he climbed in beside her.

She looked at him as he slammed the Jeep into gear. "What were you doing at the barn? Why were you in the Jeep?"

A small grin betrayed the scowl that had been fixed on his face, dimpling his right cheek. "Which question do you want me to answer first?" He turned the Jeep in a tight circle and pointed it toward the house.

"Either."

"I was at the barn, looking for you. And if I hadn't found you there, I was about to put the Jeep into four-wheel drive and head toward Turtle Creek."

She looked out the window as they drove past the irrigation pond. The water level was already rising, filling the concrete enclosure with runoff from the storm. "Why didn't you just ask Cassie where I was? She knew I had gone to the barn."

"The house was unlocked but she wasn't there."

"I thought she'd still be—"

"There was a note scribbled on the top of an empty pizza box," Jesse interrupted. "Something about going for a drive and—hands?"

"Hans," Lauren corrected. Now it made perfect sense. "I don't understand, though. Why were you going to go to Turtle Creek?"

Jesse lifted his hands off the steering wheel in a gesture of defeat. "It was the only place I could think of that you might have gone." He sounded irritated.

"But you couldn't have gotten past the barbed wire fence in the Jeep, remember?"

He stopped in front of the house and looked at her, his eyes boring into hers. "Want to make a bet?"

An image of Jesse bursting through the tight strands of barbed wire in his Jeep, looking for her in the storm, brought a swell of emotion that genuinely made her head swim.

Oh God, she loved him. It was true. And the worst thing of all was that she wanted, needed him to love her back.

The rain was pelting the windows with such force that it was impossible to see outside, and for a moment Lauren was tempted to stay there—surrounded by the aroma of the Jeep's leather interior and the woodsy smell of Jesse's damp skin. The storm lent her a welcome sense of unreality, one that made her feelings for him seem more rational.

But they couldn't stay there.

Jesse reached across her and unlatched her door. His arm brushed against hers as he straightened. His skin was warm, and his touch added a new flash of desire to the flame that was already glowing inside her. Another bolt of lightning lit the inside of the Jeep. Like the flash from a camera, it brought her back to the moment.

"This is no ordinary storm, Lauren." Jesse's voice was deep and liquid. "We need to get inside. Are you ready?"

She nodded.

"Go," he said.

She heard him unlatch his door as she flung hers open, and together they ran toward the shelter of the front porch, Jesse's hand pressed firmly between her shoulder blades.

She reached the front door first, and pushed it open so quickly that it thudded against the inside wall. Jesse shoved it closed again, shutting out the noise of the storm and the muted daylight that had managed to pierce the clouds. It was suddenly another world, dark and still and safe.

No longer in a hurry, she stood next to Jesse in the semidarkness, not knowing what to do next.

His voice penetrated the silence. "Do you have a towel I could dry off on?" He looked down at his dripping jeans. "I'm ruining your hardwood floor."

"Hold on," she called over her shoulder as she sprinted toward the laundry nook, leaving a watery trail of her own across the foyer and the kitchen floor.

She returned with two towels that she'd pulled from the dryer, a lingering warmth still clinging to the cotton.

"Thanks." He tugged a towel from her arms and buried his face in it before running it across his hair and chest.

Lauren temporarily forgot to use her own towel, mesmerized by watching Jesse. She ached with wanting him, loving him despite herself.

"I'm still dripping." His hand rested against the button of his jeans, just above the zipper. "Would it bother you if I slipped out of these? I promise I—"

An alarm blared from the top floor of the house, suspending Jesse's words. The noise finally stopped, replaced by static and the unintelligible sound of a man's voice.

"That's my weather alert," Lauren said, already heading up the stairs.

She entered her dark but familiar bedroom without hesitation and walked to her nightstand. She turned the volume down, decreasing the blare so that the announcer could be understood.

Jesse moved to stand behind her, and the announcer's words ceased to matter. She could feel the heat radiating off his body, branding her from behind. His very breathing teased her, begging her to turn and place her hand against his bare chest, to feel him, to count the steady beats of his heart.

"It sounds like the worst of it's passed," he said as the report ended. He stepped around her and parted the sheer curtains. Thunder boomed, more distant now. "It does look like it's headed east."

"That's good." Lauren felt cast in stone. Her longing for him was so real, she couldn't think of anything else. Surely he could feel it. She blotted rainwater from her face, relieved that her expression was hidden for a moment behind the towel.

Jesse let the curtain fall back into place and turned toward her. The glare from the window outlined his face and shoulders, but hid his expression from her in the dark room. "You scared the hell out of me this afternoon." His voice sounded slightly breathless and full of concern. For her? The thought made her chest constrict. No, she chided herself. She was only imagining what she wanted to hear.

She rubbed the towel across her wet hair, then draped it around her neck. "I'm sorry. I never meant to."

Without warning, he grabbed the two ends of the

towel and pulled her to him. He twisted the material in his fists until her body was nestled against his chest and hips, her neck arched against the pull of the towel. He lowered his head and kissed the hollow of her neck, flicking his tongue against her rain-slick skin in a lover's promise of what could be.

His mouth traveled upward, kissing, teasing until his lips met hers. He caught her lower lip gently between his teeth and sucked it into his mouth.

When he pulled back, his breathing was labored. "I want you, Lauren."

She felt the heady truth of his words as he held her. His readiness was unmistakable, even through the wet denim of his jeans. Knife-sharp desire pierced her, and she felt her body begin to tremble.

"I know," was all she could manage to say.

He cupped her face in his hands. "Say you want me too."

It was as if someone else stepped into her body, someone bold and daring. Lauren wrapped her arms around his neck and pulled his head to hers. "I want you too," she whispered against his mouth.

And she did. All her life she'd only taken calculated risks, told herself that timing and protocol were most important. But she was wiser now. She'd rediscovered herself in the land, in her dream, and now she wanted to make love to Jesse McCain, to steal a little of his warmth and daring, finish losing her cautious spirit in his strength.

He tugged the hem of her shirt free of her shorts, and she held her arms up, like an obedient child, as he pulled it over her head. She'd never felt this free, this uninhibited.

She wasn't a virgin. She'd made love with Roger, but the experience had only left her feeling frustrated, longing for something more. She knew it wouldn't be that way with Jesse. She knew he would fill her—body and soul.

His hands fit her perfectly as they pushed her shorts past her hips, then returned to encircle her waist. In two breaths her bra fell to the floor. Jesse stepped back, looking at her in a way that should have embarrassed her, but didn't.

She walked forward with the surreal confidence that was beginning to feel like a natural part of her, and undid the button of his jeans.

He caught her hands in his and thrust them behind her back, stepping even closer to her. She heard her own gasp as her nipples brushed against his bare chest. Holding her hands firmly with one of his own, he circled her waist with his other arm and kissed her, his tongue dipping and caressing her mouth until her knees buckled and she sank against the mattress behind her.

Jesse released her as she fell against the bed, and stood over her, waiting. Lauren let the image of him burn into her memory. He looked like a fantasy standing in her near-dark bedroom, the smooth muscles of his chest reflecting the waning daylight, his hand pausing on the zipper of his jeans.

She reached out to him, her fingers trembling with her need.

He pushed his jeans to the floor and took her outstretched hand, entwining his fingers in hers. Naked, he lowered one knee to the downy soft mattress before he covered her body with his, pinning her against the bed.

His hands captured hers again and pulled them above

her head. He felt like liquid fire on top of her, as his long, muscled legs slid against hers, edging them apart. The sensitive flesh on the insides of their arms fused where it met, and Lauren felt her nipples harden, trapped beneath his chest.

"Jesse . . ." she whispered.

In answer, he trailed his hand down her body until she thought she'd die with the need to touch him as he was touching her.

He grasped the underside of her knee, gently inching it up until she could feel his hardness brushing against her. He leaned back, his eyes searching hers in the dim light.

"Say you want this, Lauren." His expression was taut with restraint, with desire. "Say you want me."

"I want you." She bit her lip to keep it from quivering, as she watched the desire he held in check register on his face.

The words had barely left her mouth when he entered her, filling her with his thickness until a small cry escaped from her. She'd never imagined she could feel this way, this complete.

Lauren felt her blood rush to her face as he began to move inside her, long, easy strokes that fanned a desire so strong, it was frightening. She looked up, and found him watching her face.

"I've wanted you so long," he whispered as he finally released her hands, "that it seems like forever."

Her hands traveled down his arms, then his chest—hungry to touch him as he'd touched her. But as he thrust harder inside her, she stilled, her nails digging into the flesh of his sides.

He reached beneath their bodies, cupping her buttocks with one broad hand while his other hand pressed into the flesh just below her navel. With excruciating slowness, his hand traveled downward until his thumb parted her woman's lips, setting off a firework's display of light behind her eyes.

He moved his thumb in tight circles as he lifted her hips higher, fitting her against him. She felt him grow harder, thicker within her, tightening the fit of their joining, until she began to spiral upward in the darkness. He thrust one last time, burying himself as deeply as he could inside her.

She shut her eyes as the darkness lifted, leaving swirling points of lights in its place.

"Jesse," she moaned as she found her release.

She felt him go rigid and instinctively knew it was time, even before she felt the warm liquid pulse of his release.

They lay still for a long time, their bodies still joined in perfect union. Finally Jesse kissed her sleepily and pulled away, wrapping them in the rumpled comforter, then nestling her against him.

He lifted her hair to place a soft kiss against the back of her neck. "I knew it would be that way the first time I laid eyes on you."

She turned in his arms to look at him, running a finger along his cheekbone and down the jaw that had flexed in anger when he'd seen her with Ted Clarke. "I think I knew it too," she said.

He pulled her to him, again, and she shut her eyes, relishing the peaceful feeling.

The ringing of the phone cut through the silence. When Lauren opened her eyes, the shadows in the room had deepened. The phone rang a second time, and she swore under her breath, struggling to free her arms from the comforter. Finally, she leaned over Jesse and pulled the receiver from the cradle of the phone.

"Hello." She hoped she didn't sound as if she'd just been making love.

"Miss Adams, this is Leo Harbison with the highway department," the voice on the other end of the phone stated. "My secretary said you called earlier."

"Yes, I did, Mr. Harbison." She sat up and tucked her hair behind her ear. "I was hoping the status of the project had changed since the coin was found."

There was a pause before Mr. Harbison spoke again. "I'm afraid I don't know what you're talking about. To the best of my knowledge, no artifact from your site has been turned in."

The mattress shifted as Jesse sat up. Before Lauren knew what was happening, he'd jerked the receiver from her hand.

"Leo? Hello. This is Jesse McCain. I just overheard your conversation with Miss Adams and thought I'd set the record straight." He glanced at Lauren and looked quickly away again. "I came across a metal fragment yesterday that I'd hoped was a coin. It turns out it was only an old button of some sort." He shook his head as he listened. "No, nothing of any significance."

Lauren couldn't make sense of what she was hearing. Jesse hadn't turned in the artifact? He'd told her he was taking it directly to the university for lab analysis. Her ears began to ring as a sick feeling of betrayal settled in the pit of her stomach.

Jesse chuckled into the receiver. "I wish I were that lucky, Leo. No, Miss Adams has simply been kind enough to let me use her facilities from time to time. I

just happened to overhear her conversation with you."
He nodded, smiling. "You too. I'll be in touch."

She stared at Jesse, searching his face for some hint
of explanation. *Kind enough to let me use her facilities?*
Obviously he had been trying to explain away his presence in her house, but his words had a disturbing ring of
truth to them. She shifted uncomfortably. Her body was
still moist and sore from their lovemaking. She tugged
the sheet over her bare breasts, momentarily at a loss for
words.

Jesse turned to her. "I know that was bad timing, but
I had to—"

"Why did you lie to him?" she interrupted. She
scrambled off the bed, taking the sheet with her, and
switched on the lamp next to the phone. "Why didn't
you turn the coin in?"

A dark expression crossed his face. "Didn't you think
I'd figure it out, Lauren?"

His words didn't make sense, but she had the feeling
she was being accused of something, and that was a feeling she knew all too well. It had happened countless
times on her old job. Turn the blame around, make
Lauren feel responsible for someone else's lack of com-
petence, of integrity.

Jesse was becoming a stranger before her eyes. She
backed toward her rocking chair and fumbled for her
robe, which she'd left lying across it. Had she really
drifted off to sleep in this man's arms moments before?
She shrugged into the robe, immediately feeling better
once the thick belt was securely tied around her waist.

"Figure what out?" she asked.

He reached over the side of the bed for his underwear and pulled it on. "That you planted the coin."

Chill bumps ran in waves across her body as she took in the meaning of his words. Planted the coin? "Jesse, you were there when I found it!"

He grasped her shoulders and looked into her face. "I know you felt desperate, but other people could have been hurt by your little scheme."

"Little scheme?" Lauren wiggled out of his grip. She picked up his still-damp jeans and threw them at him, hitting him in the stomach. "The only scheme I see here is yours. Let me guess. Leo told you to excavate but not to actually find any artifacts. Right?"

"I'd never agree to anything like that and you know it." Jesse's voice trembled with anger.

"No, I don't. I don't really know you at all, and that's the way it's going to stay." She breathed deep, letting her anger lend her strength. "Get dressed and get out."

He pulled his jeans into place, zipping them but leaving the top button undone. "I think we have something special. Why would you want to mess it up?"

She looked at the button of his jeans, her fingers aching to fasten it with the same tenderness as she'd undone it, but that moment was gone from her forever. And what would have been a beautiful memory was now a terrible mistake.

"You're the only one who has messed up," she said. "If you think I'm going to stand by and keep my mouth shut about what I found, you're wrong." She planted her fists on her hips. "You have something of mine, and I want it. I'll get the media involved if I have to."

"Dammit," he muttered, "that's the last thing any of us need. There would be repercussions beyond what you know, Lauren."

She threw her hands in the air. "Stop pretending

with me, Jesse. I know how the politics of these things work."

"Has it occurred to you that I didn't turn the coin in because I didn't want to see you get into trouble any more than I want to wash my career down the drain?"

"Save your concern for somebody who's naive enough to believe it." Her heart hurt as the words left her mouth. She'd not only been naive enough to believe he was concerned about her, but had fallen in love with him for it.

He headed for the door of her bedroom. "Try thanking your lucky stars that someone was there to stop you from getting yourself in any deeper."

She suppressed a sense of alarm at the sight of him actually leaving. No, she wouldn't fall apart now.

"Either you turn it in, or I'll blow the whistle," she stated, her voice devoid of the emotion that was boiling just below her skin.

He stopped at the door and turned to face her. "Go ahead and do that then. It will be your word against mine." He walked through the doorway, everything but the sound of his footsteps disappearing into the shadows.

Lauren didn't waste any time after the front door slammed behind him before jerking the sheets from the bed and showering. She was in a hurry to wash away the traces of their lovemaking. But after throwing the sheets in the washer and lathering every inch of herself in the shower, she began to cry. She gave in to the need, crying for the loss of what could have been, until she found herself leaning against the tile, exhausted but at least temporarily absolved from the heartache she felt.

She mustered the strength to pour Lucky a dish of dry dog food before making her way back up the stairs and crawling into bed. She hugged her pillow against her chest, and hoped that her ability to sleep through any crisis wouldn't fail her. Her pillow was scratchy without its case, and she didn't bother with a blanket, but her thick terry-cloth robe protected her from the air-conditioning as she drifted off.

When she opened her eyes next, it was morning and she was filled with a strange buzz of energy. She knew she should feel wretched instead, but didn't question her luck. Instead she put fresh sheets on the bed, cleaned the tub . . . and organized the toiletries on top of her bathroom counter and put another load of clothes in the wash. The next thing she knew, she had vacuumed the entire house and was stripping wax from the kitchen floor when the doorbell rang.

She was as certain as she knew her own name that it wasn't Jesse, but she peeped through the side window of the door just to be certain. It was Cassie. Lauren pasted on her best smile and opened the door.

"Why was the door still locked?" Cassie threw her hand over her nose as she stepped over the threshold. "Good Lord, what is that?"

"Ammonia. I'm mopping the floor."

Cassie stepped back and looked Lauren up and down. "You're in your bathrobe, and it's ten o'clock in the morning. Shouldn't you be in your overalls feeding the chickens or something?"

She chose to ignore her sister's sarcasm, and walked back toward the kitchen. "You're right, I shouldn't still be in my robe." She picked up the sponge mop and thrust it into Cassie's hands. "So I'll leave you to finish up while I go get dressed."

"Hey!" Cassie called after her as she bounded up the stairs. "I don't know how to work this thing."

"It goes back and forth, back and forth. You'll get the hang of it."

"If you're not back down here in five minutes, I'm going to change my mind," Cassie shouted over the rhythmic squeaking of the mop.

Lauren crossed her fingers. Cassie could only mean she'd changed her mind about working with Ted's horse. Lauren slipped on a pair of blue jean shorts and a tank top, pulled her hair into a ponytail, and flew back down the stairs.

She peeked around the doorway to find a disgruntled-looking Cassie pushing the mop with her thumb and index finger, as if some flesh-eating bacteria might jump onto her arm. "You'll do it then?" Lauren asked.

Cassie rolled her eyes. "Yes, on one condition."

"What's that?"

"I do it alone. No mopey man and no sad-eyed kid. You got it?"

"Okay, sure. But Ted really seems like a nice man, and I'm sure his daughter is—"

"A clinging vine. I don't need it, Lauren." She handed the mop back to her sister. "You promise?"

"I promise." Lauren hugged Cassie, and the mop oozed water onto Cassie's expensive leather pumps.

"Lauren!" Cassie moaned.

"Oh, I'm sorry." She released her sister and straightened. "There is one more thing, Sis," she said hesitantly.

Cassie hopped on one foot, shaking the mop water out of her shoe. "You're in a brave mood."

"It's nothing really." Lauren wondered if her sister would detect the serious tone that had crept into her voice. She could hear it, but then she knew just how serious the situation had become since Jesse had refused to turn in the coin. She also knew she was grasping at straws. "I was just wondering if you'd help me look for Grandmother's arrowheads."

Cassie frowned. "I haven't thought about them in years."

"Don't you remember? She kept them in that old brass container in the study. But I can't find them. I've searched all over."

Cassie glanced at her watch. "I have time before my next appointment, as long as I don't get too dirty." She looked pointedly at her wet shoes. "But why do you want to dig them out?"

Lauren thought her face would crack from maintaining a nonchalant expression. "I thought they might be helpful to Jesse." Saying his name out loud caused her stomach to roll, and she clenched the mop handle tighter to keep her hands from trembling.

"Wait, I'm confused." Cassie looked suspicious. "I thought that old coin was the answer to your prayers."

"Oh, I'm sure it will be," Lauren said as she walked through the foyer and opened the front door, setting the mop and bucket on the front porch. She glanced toward the meadow, wondering if Jesse would have the nerve to show up.

Yes, the coin would be the answer to her prayers, she thought. If she ever got her hands on it again.

Every muscle in Jesse's body protested as he stood and stretched. He turned his well-worn trowel over and over in his hands, his gaze automatically falling to the curve of the old logging road. The only activity was the premature blinking of a lightning bug.

He had fully expected Lauren to forbid him access to her land that morning, so he'd decided not to press his luck and had parked up the road from her house. Still, he'd kept one eye on the logging road as the day had stretched on, anticipating—half-hoping—to see her marching toward him to finish their argument.

She hadn't, though. So he'd done the only thing he knew to do, and that was to begin excavating the creek site. It was ridiculous to consider that the coin might be for real. It was even more ridiculous to attempt an excavation—no matter how small—alone. But there was no way he could justify asking for additional help without telling his superiors about the coin.

Jesse massaged the back of his neck with his free hand. The truth was, no matter how hard he tried, he couldn't convince himself to ignore the possibilities. So he'd pushed himself, making sketches and stringing off the site in the usual grid pattern that would organize the dig.

It had been maddening, preparing the site alone. And to make matters worse, his mind had kept playing tricks on him. Several times he'd thought he'd heard Lauren's voice, but when he had looked up, no one was there. He shut his eyes, remembering yesterday—the sweet scent of her skin, the dampness he'd discovered between her legs. She had wanted him just as much as he'd wanted her.

Jesse felt himself growing hard at the thought, and cursed under his breath.

He hadn't expected the uninhibited passion that

she'd revealed, and memories of it haunted him. He'd spent as much time fighting the fresh waves of desire that hit him whenever he recalled their lovemaking, as he had fighting the sweltering heat of the day.

He looked at the moist, exposed earth in the square he'd been digging, and shook his head. There was no way, no way in hell, that the coin had come from this site. Still, all day long he'd found himself eyeing the oddly shaped raised area, wishing that he'd find something that proved Lauren hadn't lied to him after all.

Behind him, a katydid called out, and he jumped at the unexpected trilling noise. He looked around him, noticing for the first time how late it was. He glanced at his watch, and found that he couldn't make out the time until he punched the nighttime mode that lit the dial. Eight o'clock. No wonder he was so damned hungry.

The light had faded gradually, and his eyes had apparently adjusted to the change without him realizing it. But now the sun had dipped completely below the hills of the valley, and it was difficult to see. He ground the heel of his mud-caked boot in frustration. He still had work to do. At least there was a night breeze rolling into the valley, swirling a ghostly white mist around the meadow grasses and creek banks.

Jesse dug a penlight from his equipment bag and squatted down next to the square he'd been working on. Holding the slender flashlight between his teeth, he resumed the tedious, horizontal scraping of the earth.

A twig snapped somewhere to his right, and he looked up.

"You didn't even have the good taste to wait a day or two before you came back to finish looting, did you?"

Lauren's voice interrupted the tranquil song of the crickets and the katydids.

She was standing a few feet away from him, mist swirling about her legs—and a rifle pointed straight at his head.

EIGHT

Of course she wouldn't actually shoot Jesse, but Lauren did know how to use the rifle. And even though she'd only brought it because she'd thought Lucky might be barking at a snake or a pack of wild dogs, it gave her a certain satisfaction to see the shock on Jesse's face.

The puppy started toward Jesse, but Lauren called him back with a slap against her knee. "Stay," she commanded. Lucky gave her a perplexed look and shifted from foot to foot, but stayed by her side.

She'd been wrong about men before, but she never would have thought Jesse McCain would stoop this low. She'd read about pothunters and the valuable artifacts they sold on the black market, but Jesse was a professional. They were supposed to loathe looters. But here he was, trowel in hand and his Jeep nowhere in sight. Well, so much for professional integrity.

He pulled the flashlight from his mouth, and squinted at her in the darkness. "Lauren, put that rifle down."

"Not until I hear your best version of what you're

doing here." She was surprised to hear the sarcasm in her voice when her heart felt as if it would beat out of her chest.

He stood. "What difference does it make? You're not going to believe me anyway."

"You're right," she said. "So why don't you give me the coin back right now? You can keep anything else you've found here tonight."

"Lauren, look at me." He held his arms wide. His white T-shirt was the only thing that stood out in the near darkness, and she instantly noticed the heavy streaks of dirt on it. "Would a looter go to this much trouble?" He gestured beside him at the spiderweb of white string that glowed in perfect squares against the black earth.

He had a point, but she was far from ready to believe what he had to say, and too pleased with herself to lower the rifle yet.

"I want the coin back, Jesse." She battled to control the quiver in her voice. "It's not fair and you know it. I've worked too hard to accomplish what I have. I'm not about to roll over and play dead now."

He took a step toward her. "It's not like that," he said, his voice softening.

It was getting genuinely dark now, and Lauren felt her resolve, and her bravery, faltering. "Stop," she said, shifting the rifle against her shoulder. "I want the coin back, and I want it tonight."

He worked his right hand into the front pocket of his jeans. Lauren took a deep breath, struggling not to be distracted by the image that sprang into her head—of those jeans sliding off his hips, his body naked as it had been yesterday.

When he threw the keys to her, they bumped against her thigh and fell to the ground.

She lowered the rifle and stooped to pick them up. "What's this?" she asked.

"The keys to my apartment—2900 Meadow Ridge. The coin is inside an attaché case under my bed."

She was at a loss for words. The act seemed so trusting. A lot of energy had gone into casting Jesse as the villain in this scenario, and he was stepping out of character. She glanced at the excavation grid. Could he be telling the truth?

Don't be a fool, Lauren, she told herself.

"I don't expect to see you back here again," she said, using the last of her bravado.

"You do what you have to, but I have a legal right to be here." He wiped his brow on the sleeve of his T-shirt. "It's my job."

She thrust her chin in the air. "And it's my job to look out for myself." As she turned to walk away from him, her heart gave a painful twist. "Because no one else is going to," she whispered to herself as she walked away. "That's for sure."

She welcomed the mist that enveloped her and obscured the beam of Jesse's flashlight as she headed back to the house.

Lauren was surrounded by the essence of Jesse the moment she pushed open the door to his apartment. The lingering smell of his aftershave, his field notes scattered across the kitchen table, the pair of muddy hiking boots next to the door—they were all painful reminders of the man she'd made love to only yesterday.

The apartment was in an upscale part of town, and she was surprised at how sparsely furnished it was. His sofa and love seat looked new, but there were no pictures on the walls, no plants, no family photos scattered about.

What was she doing here? It had seemed the right thing to do on the drive over. After all, he'd tried to cheat her. And he'd definitely lied to her about the coin. But her being in his home felt like such an invasion of his privacy that chill bumps ran the length of her arms. She tried rubbing them away with her hands. She was being ridiculous. It was simply cold in the air-conditioned apartment.

She forced herself to walk straight to his bedroom and look under the bed for the attaché case. She found it right away. Sitting down on the edge of the bed, she withdrew a piece of black felt. The thin silver coin fell into her hand as she unfolded the felt.

Lauren turned it over in her palm. Old things, like antiques, had always given her a strange feeling, as if for a moment time stood still. It was amazing that the coin had survived, held above the swift current of the creek by only a broken piece of pottery.

She had a brief understanding of why Jesse was suspicious of the find, but pushed it aside. He was only trying to cover for his own actions. And even if he weren't, he had no right to question her honesty.

She refolded the coin in the felt and pushed it into the front pocket of her shorts. As she started to stand, she found her hand lingering on the sheet. She hadn't thought of Jesse as the unmade-bed type, but his sheets were twisted around a dark green bedspread and shoved to the foot of the king-size mattress. One pillow was thrown against the oak headboard, another rested in the corner of the bedroom. It looked like he'd had a restless night.

All energy seemed to drain from her body, and she fought the urge to lie down on the bed—Jesse's bed. It was as if he were there in the room with her, and all she had to do was rest and let him take care of her. She tugged the pillow into her lap and hugged it against her, burying her face in the soft cotton and inhaling the scent, the essence of Jesse, in desperate gulps.

She knew that turning the coin in to Mr. Harbison would make him aware that Jesse had lied. She didn't know what would happen beyond that, but she knew she didn't have a choice.

"You can't know how sorry I am for what I'm about to do," she whispered into the pillow. "I can't even believe it myself."

"Damn." Jesse pressed the heel of his hand against his forehead as he swung his legs over the edge of the bed. "I shouldn't have listened to Ken last night."

It had been years since he'd gotten really drunk, and now he remembered why. It felt like someone was whacking him across the skull with a baseball bat.

He'd left the excavation site dead tired and confused. Lauren wasn't acting like someone who'd been caught trying to deceive him. In fact, her little theatrical attempt to turn the tables on him had looked pretty real. He rubbed his fingers against his temples. The rifle had looked pretty real too.

As usual, Ken had been there to offer him a shower and a distraction. He just wished now that he hadn't found the distraction in the bottom of a bottle of tequila.

But the burning sensation in his gut wasn't only from the alcohol. Something else was eating him, and even through the haze of his hangover, he knew what it was.

He didn't care if Lauren had planted the coin.

Hell, it probably hadn't even occurred to her that such a stunt could cost him his job. And even if she did know about the failed Coosa expedition, she would have no way of knowing the toll it had taken on Luke Ebsin. She'd been scared and desperate. And pretty resourceful, too, he had to admit.

Standing, he decided, had been a bad idea, but he needed to get to the kitchen—and to a cup of coffee. Even if the room was spinning.

After two cups of the strong, hot liquid he began to feel more human. A cool shower and a breakfast of dry toast later, he decided he wanted to live after all.

He'd opened his eyes that morning knowing he'd been wrong to judge Lauren for planting the artifact, especially when he hadn't told her the truth about the interchange project to begin with. That revelation had since turned into a burning need to come clean, to confess.

He was shaved, dressed, and out the door in record time, making up for his sluggish start. Now his Jeep couldn't take the curves on the twisted country road fast enough. God, he wanted to see her, wanted to make her understand.

His chest constricted so tightly that for a moment he wondered if something was physically wrong with him. He held his breath, but his thoughts raced forward. What if he couldn't make her understand? As stubborn as she was, she might never forgive him for deceiving her.

The thought that he might lose her for good made him grip the steering wheel so hard, it made a plastic popping sound, warning him to lighten up. He tried to calm down, to tell himself that his confession was no more urgent than it had been from the start. Still, he had a nagging feeling in his gut.

Besides, he hadn't been in love with her then.

He almost pulled off onto the shoulder of the road at that thought, but he kept driving, his arms wood-stiff against the wheel. You love her? an inner voice asked. Jesse McCain who'd been set adrift by his own parents—a loner, a wanderer. What did he know about love, about making someone else happy?

He felt moisture beading on his forehead and willed his fingers to relax, then his hands and shoulders, until finally he was back in control and the inner voice was silenced. A weak smile crossed his face. Yes, he loved her. And he'd learn how to make her happy if it took him the rest of his life. If their lovemaking was any indication, he already knew one way.

When he turned onto the single-lane road that led to Lauren's house, he began to feel better, lighter—as if he'd stripped blinders from his eyes.

As he rounded the curve of the driveway, he noticed Cassie working a small bay horse on a lunge line in the paddock. That's a surprise, he thought as he parked his Jeep between the barn and a big blue Cadillac. He watched her expertly maneuvering the horse around her in a wide circle. So much for having her pegged as a die-hard city girl, he thought, and opened the Jeep door.

Jesse walked to the paddock. "Cassie?" he called over the fence.

Cassie clicked her tongue to the horse, ignoring him.

"Canter," she commanded as she looked in Jesse's direction and cracked the lunge whip. It swished in the air several feet behind the horse, its snapping sound her only response.

Well, judging from the welcome, she probably shared Lauren's opinion of him right now. Which meant Lauren had told her everything. He steeled himself for a confrontation, and decided to try the direct approach. "Is Lauren around?" he asked.

"No." She cracked the whip again, unnecessarily, he thought, since the horse was already in a fast canter.

"I need to talk to her. It's important." He raised his voice to be heard over the beating of the horse's hooves against the packed dirt. "Where is she?"

"Slow," Cassie told the horse, and waited for him to slow to an easy jog before she turned her attention to Jesse. "She has a lunch date. I don't know when she'll be back."

Jesse felt as if someone had punched him in the stomach. "Whose horse are you working?"

He thought he saw the hint of a smile on Cassie's face before she answered. "Ted Clarke's."

Now he was sure where he'd seen the Cadillac before. "She's with him, isn't she?"

Cassie moved the long whip in front of the small horse and commanded, "Whoa," tapping him on the chest as he slowed to a stop. She turned to Jesse, her blond eyebrows lowered in a serious frown. "It's none of your business who she's with."

Jesse opened the paddock gate and walked through. "I have to talk to her, Cassie."

"I don't see any reason why I should tell you where she is." Cassie gathered the lunge line and pulled the horse to her side. It danced in place as Jesse approached. "Easy, boy." She patted him on the neck.

"Dammit, Cassie, tell me where she is." With a sudden motion, he lifted one hand to comb it through his hair. "You're wrong about what's going on. . . ."

The horse began backing away, and Cassie struggled to keep her footing. "Jesse, quit it. You're scaring the horse."

A firm hand clasped him on the shoulder, and Jesse turned to find himself looking into Ted Clarke's angry eyes.

"Yes, he is scaring the horse, and he's being just as big a jackass as he was before." Ted raised his eyebrows, then smiled. "It looks to me like the lady doesn't have anything to say to you."

Jesse knocked Ted's hand from his shoulder, and for a moment he thought the other man was going to take a shot at him.

He didn't, though. Instead Ted lowered his voice and jabbed his finger at Jesse's chest. "Look, I know love can do strange things to a guy, but it's going to get you damaged if you don't get a grip on yourself."

Jesse wasn't thrilled about having the other man in his face, but there was a definite ring of truth to what he said, both about acting like a jackass and being in love. Was it that obvious or was this guy just very perceptive? He dropped his eyes, thinking now was as good a time as any to apologize.

"You're right," he said, looking back at Ted. "And I'm sorry about the other day." Jesse extended his hand, and Ted accepted it with a genuine smile.

"Hey, if you two are through male bonding," Cassie called out, "I have something I'd like to say to Jesse."

Jesse looked at her.

"Get lost," she said, then she led the horse from the paddock and tied him to a hitching post near the barn door.

"I'm sorry, Cassie," Jesse said, mustering every ounce of his patience. "But if you won't tell me where Lauren is, then will you at least give her a message?"

Cassie rubbed the horse down with a dry towel for at least two minutes before she finally looked up at him, leaning her elbows across the horse's back. "I'm not her secretary. But if you want to leave her a note, the house isn't locked."

Jesse started to thank her, but couldn't quite bring his lips to form the words. He walked toward the house instead. He'd find a way to mend that bridge later. After all, it looked like Cassie and Lauren were a package deal.

As he reached the door to the house, Cassie's voice rang out. "Just don't lift the family silver, will ya?"

Jesse found a pen in the kitchen, but couldn't find a blank sheet of paper. He remembered seeing a study on the second floor, so he headed up the stairs and down the wide hall.

The hardwood floor of the hallway gleamed, and he noticed that there were no spiderwebs in the corners of the nine-foot ceilings. He glanced into Lauren's bedroom as he passed. The bed was made, several lacy throw pillows perfectly arranged on the white comforter. Between the upkeep of the rambling old farmhouse and the stable renovations, Lauren should be about ready to drop from exhaustion.

No wonder she'd gone out on a limb and bought the coin, he mused. She was probably too tired to think straight.

He found the study as tidy as the rest of the house, and there was a notepad positioned next to Lauren's appointment calendar. Appointment calendar. He picked it up, scanning it for the day's date. In the space for June 28th, Lauren had written in neat cursive writing, "Birmingham—Caffè Italiano. Meet Mr. Harbison at 11:30."

His first reaction was relief. She wasn't on a date after all. She was only meeting Mr. Harbison. Then he remembered that she had the coin. Jesse banged his fist on the desk, sending a dish of paper clips flying through the air. The colorful plastic clips scattered all across the polished wood.

The little imp was going to cause more trouble than she could possibly imagine. What was worse, if Leo didn't recognize the coin as a fraud, he might alert the university. Then there would be no stopping a full-scale excavation. No stopping Luke from getting involved. Jesse looked at his watch—11:15.

It would take at least thirty minutes to get to Birmingham, but Leo Harbison had been late for every appointment Jesse had ever had with the man. He dashed down the hall, trying not to slip on the polished hardwood floor.

He hoped Leo was running late today.

Lauren tapped the toe of her navy pump against the checkered tile of the restaurant floor, and glanced at her watch again. She'd been waiting for fifteen minutes. She looked over her shoulder toward the entrance. Where was Mr. Harbison?

Opening her purse, she unfolded the black felt, making sure the coin was still safely tucked inside. It was. She sighed, trying not to question what she was about to do.

As soon as she put the coin back and snapped her purse closed, a strong hand grasped her upper arm. She turned, expecting to see Mr. Harbison, but found herself looking at a denim-clad thigh instead.

Jesse. Her gaze traveled up the length of his body until it rested on his face.

His hair was pulled back into its customary short ponytail, which accentuated the angry V of his eyebrows. The rapid rise and fall of his chest was obvious from her vantage point.

"Come with me." He tugged on her arm.

"I'm not going anywhere," she snapped. "Get your hand off me."

"You're lucky I beat Leo here." Jesse raised her to her feet. Lauren looked around her, and found several of the other customers in the quiet little restaurant openly staring at them. "Now come on before he shows up."

"I'm waiting on him to show up, you brute," she whispered angrily as she jerked her arm from his grasp. "What do you think you're doing here?"

"I'm saving you from answering a lot of questions that could get you into trouble." He wove his fingers through hers and tugged on her hand. "If you don't want to cause a scene, then close your mouth and follow me."

They were already causing a scene. Lauren's face grew hot, and she knew from experience that it was glowing, bright red, from all the whispers and stares of the customers. They probably thought she regularly put up with this type of manhandling.

She decided her best course of action was to go out-side, then give Jesse a piece of her mind. She smiled for the benefit of the people in the restaurant, and followed him toward the exit.

Just as they reached it an older man entered the res-taurant and waved at them.

"Leo," she heard Jesse say as he dropped her hand. "Listen, something has come up at the test excavation I'm doing on the Adams property, so Lauren can't meet with you now."

Jesse clasped her on the shoulder and nudged her forward. Lauren found herself smiling at Leo Harbison for lack of any other sane response to the situation. What was she going to do, yell, "Help, I'm being kid-napped!"?

Her mind was whirling. This was *her* appointment, designed to blow the whistle on Jesse's little scam, but here she stood, paralyzed by the warm touch of his hand on her shoulder and flooded with relief that she hadn't turned him in.

Jesse pumped the other man's hand. "I'm afraid we have to get going, but I'll call you if we have any news."

With that Jesse pushed her out the door and into the blinding daylight—where no one was watching and there were no more appearances to maintain.

She threw Jesse's hand from her shoulder and socked him with her purse. "How dare you!" she yelled.

"Don't be tossing that purse around like that. There's a sixteenth-century artifact in there." He reached to take her hand again. "You and I need to have a talk."

"Oh, no, you don't," she said as she jerked her hand

away. "I'm leaving." She pulled her car keys from her purse.

"Lauren, wait." Jesse caught up with her and grasped her shoulder, dangling his own keys in front of her. "I'm driving, and you're going to be my passenger." He touched the side of her face and smiled. "My silent passenger. I have a lot I need to say to you."

Silent passenger, her ass! She'd had that job before, and never intended to return to it. She smiled sweetly, grabbed his keys, and tossed them into the drainage ditch that bordered the parking lot.

"Lauren!" he yelled. "What the hell did you do that for?"

"I don't intend to be anybody's silent anything," she said as she sauntered to her car. She climbed in, locked the door behind her, then looked in her rearview mirror as she pulled out of the parking lot. Jesse stood in the same spot, his hands resting on his hips, shaking his head.

Only then did she begin to tremble with rage and . . . She pressed her fingers against the hollow of her neck, remembering the tender kisses Jesse had placed there just a day ago. It was impossible to define the bittersweet emotions she felt for him. They seemed to literally assault her body, her senses.

She recalled the brush of his bare hips against hers, the silken hardness of his body entering hers. The way his neck smelled when she'd nuzzled against it. A half sob, half laugh escaped her as she remembered him standing in her kitchen that first day, a pink gingham dish towel thrown across one shoulder while he fried bacon.

When Lauren pulled into her driveway, she was almost shocked to see she was home. It was as if she'd driven there on remote control. She recalled every painful image of Jesse that had entered her mind as she drove, but not the interstate, the traffic, or the country roads that led to the farm.

Muscles tightened across her shoulders and neck as she spotted the now-familiar blue Cadillac parked next to the barn. She was going to catch hell from Cassie for that unexpected visit. But when she looked closer, she saw Ted and Cassie leaning against the paddock gate, their heads bowed close to each other's as they watched the feisty little gelding at play.

"Well, aren't y'all cozy?" she whispered.

She got out of the car and waved a greeting, though she had no intention of speaking. Cassie had an annoying habit of getting the upper hand in any situation, and lately it was all Lauren could do to keep from getting trampled.

She smiled despite herself. Ted Clarke might be good for her flighty sister. She thought about the sadness that haunted his eyes. Come to think of it, Cassie might be good for him too.

She'd broken her best suit out of storage that morning, and when she'd first put it on, it had made her feel capable and smart. Now it made her feel hot and defeated. She jerked her pumps from her feet and walked barefoot across the warm concrete driveway, not caring what damage she did to her stockings.

Men wore nice, comfortable shoes, whether they were blue-collar or white-collar workers. Women wore instruments of torture. Just one of many injustices, she thought as she slung open the front door and stepped inside.

The air-conditioning was an instant, welcome relief. She tossed her purse onto the kitchen table and shrugged out of her suit coat. A tall, icy glass of lemonade and a nap were what she needed. She'd stared at the digital clock on her dresser until two-thirty in the morning, trying to convince herself that giving Leo Harbison the coin was the right thing to do. Now she felt like she could sleep for a week.

She looked around for a sheet of paper, but couldn't find one. Finally, in a fit of temper, she tore the cover from the telephone book and with a felt-tip marker wrote, "QUIET—SISTER SLEEPING" on the blank side.

Lauren spent the last of her energy pouring the glass of lemonade and jogging up the stairs to her bedroom. She propped the makeshift sign against the doorframe, and closed and locked her bedroom door behind her. If only she could shut out the world—and her problems—that easily.

She felt trapped inside the hot businesslike shirt and lined skirt she wore, and wasted no time getting out of them. Once her panty hose landed in the far corner of the bedroom, she finally felt free again. After rummaging through her drawers for a minute, she came up with the perfect attire—an oversize undershirt she'd swiped from her father on her last visit.

Nope, no frilly sleepwear for her this afternoon. Those were designed to make her feel like a woman, and she knew no matter how hard she fought it, she would eventually wind up thinking of Jesse. And right now the last thing she wanted to think about was Jesse.

She switched the overhead fan on low, climbed on top of the bed, and took a long swig of the lemonade.

Her life had definitely taken a strange turn lately. She leaned her head back against the pillow and shut her eyes. She wished she'd never heard of the beltway, and for all the trouble it had caused her, she was beginning to wish she'd never found the coin.

But even though her heart felt like it would break in two, she didn't regret meeting Jesse. Her life before seemed painfully dull in comparison. She set the lemonade on the bed stand with an angry thud. Why did he have to turn out to be just another liar?

No, don't think about it, she told herself. Instead she imagined him ankle-deep in polluted ditch water, feeling the slimy bottom of the ditch for his car keys. She smiled to herself, recalling the way his self-satisfied expression had melted when she'd tossed the keys into the ditch. She laughed out loud. Hey, maybe this was what they meant by self-therapy. Or was it regression therapy? No, self-hypnosis. She took another swig of lemonade. Whatever it was, she was feeling better already.

She jerked at the sudden pounding on her bedroom door, sloshing lemonade out of her glass and dribbling it down her chin to the front of her shirt. Was Cassie trying to scare the life out of her? As she struggled to swallow the overspill of lemonade in her mouth, the pounding started up again. Didn't her sister see the note?

"Lauren, if you don't open up in three seconds, I'm going to break this door down." Jesse's voice echoed in the quiet of the old house.

Lauren choked on the lemonade, and the tangy liquid burned her eyes and throat like acid. Jesse? Impossible! He was supposed to be knee-deep in sludge right now.

"Lauren, answer me." The voice on the other side of the door sounded like it meant business.

"Go away," she said, her own voice squeaky, still tight from swallowing the lemonade wrong.

"Open up. I want to talk to you." He sounded calmer.

"Haven't you done enough damage?" She attempted to mop the lemonade from her shirt, trying to ignore the heavy pounding of her pulse.

"Yes, I have. But if you'll hear me out, I'll try to explain."

"No," she answered.

"Well, the way I see it, you don't have a choice." The door creaked against its hinges, and she heard Jesse settling down against the other side.

Lauren felt her face flush with anger. He was right. She didn't have a choice.

"First of all," he said, "I understand about the coin. You thought planting it at the site was the only way to keep the interchange project away from your land."

Lauren picked the glass of lemonade back up, seriously considering hurling it against the door. Honestly, how could he stand to keep up the charade?

"Well, Mr. McCain, that's mighty big of you. What has you in such an understanding mood?"

She heard him shift against the door, and steeled herself for an equally sarcastic comeback.

"Because I have a confession myself," he said.

Some of her anger gave way to curiosity. So, was he finally going to admit that he had his own reasons for keeping the coin—reasons that had less to do with her and more to do with his bank account?

"I'm listening," she said when the silence stretched on.

"The highway department picked an alternate route for the interchange," he said, his voice flat. "Your land isn't in any danger."

Lauren's heart turned over in her chest. *"They picked the other route,"* she whispered to herself, stunned. She didn't have to worry anymore. Before she knew it, she was on her feet, her hands clasped against her cheeks like a child.

But something else was wrong, she could hear it in Jesse's voice. She ran her hand through her hair, trying to gather her thoughts. He'd said that he had a confession.

"Lauren?" he called to her from the other side of the door.

She felt a rush of nausea at the tension in his voice. "Yes?"

There was a long pause. Then Jesse said, "I've known all along."

NINE

He'd known all along. Lauren swallowed hard as a second wave of nausea hit her.

How stupid she must seem. And the highway department—how dare they put her through this hell! Her hands curled into fists, and she glanced around her room, the urge to throw something building until she thought she'd burst.

She unlocked the bedroom door and threw it open, its doorknob denting the Sheetrock as it slammed against the wall.

Jesse was standing, his face uncertain, his shoulders slumped in a helpless-looking posture. Helpless, her rear! He'd played her for a fool, used her body and soul.

"You son of a bitch," she growled through clenched teeth. "You black-hearted son of a bitch." Her fist hit him square in the chest, just below the last button of his polo shirt.

"Lauren, don't." Jesse stumbled backward a step and tried to grab her fist. She jerked it away. He failed to sidestep the next blow, which slammed into his right shoulder.

"You must be proud of yourself." She felt tears sliding down her cheeks. Surely she wasn't crying. She was too angry to cry.

But her throat constricted as she remembered the look of tenderness on Jesse's face when they'd made love—even when his amber-brown eyes had been lit with passion. She felt a tear drop onto her thin shirt.

"Listen to me," Jesse said, trying to cup her face in his hands.

She knocked his hands away. "If you only knew how sick I am of listening to lying men, you wouldn't have the nerve to be standing in front of me."

"I couldn't tell you the truth." He smoothed back a strand of his hair that had escaped from his ponytail. "Do you hear me? I wasn't allowed to tell anyone, especially you."

She was so disgusted by it all. Did they enjoy taking advantage of women in general, or was it just her? She'd never thought of herself as weak, but here she was again, made a fool of by a bunch of fat politicians and the good ol' boy network at the highway department.

"Let me take a wild guess. . . ." Her laughter rang hollow in the empty hallway. "The *system* made you lie to me." . . . *and make love to me, and make me fall in love with you.* "Well, the system can go to hell and take you with it!"

She felt her temper building again, pulsing beneath her flesh until it was ready to spin out of control. She had to do something, so she flattened her hands against Jesse's chest and pushed with every ounce of energy she could muster. She needed to shut him back out—put the barrier of the door between them again.

He caught her wrists, though, and pulled her toward him until he cradled her hands, still balled into fists, just below his chin. "You're going to listen to me if I have to sit on you." His words were even, despite his rapid breathing.

When he brushed his lips against her knuckles, Lauren considered bringing her knee up between his legs. Until she made the mistake of meeting his eyes. There it was, the warmth, the kindness that had made her trust him, lose her heart to him in the first place.

"I know I hurt you, Lauren," he said. "But I couldn't tell you until I was certain I could trust you, and then—"

"Thanks. Your loyalty astounds me," Lauren said sarcastically.

His brows came together as his eyes narrowed. "My loyalty has always had to be to myself first." He dropped her hands and looked away. "That's how you survived in my family. But what would you know about it?"

"Oh, I know about loyalty, Jesse." She folded her arms across her chest, her fists still balled. "And I know even more about it now. I put my trust in you, when I should have been protecting my home."

He leaned against the doorframe, his own hands flexing into fists. "I know how you must feel. I know you only wanted to protect your home."

"Do you? How could you, Jesse?"

He straightened then, his eyes boring into hers. "Maybe I don't know what it feels like to want to protect your home, but I know what it feels like to want a home."

Lauren shivered. The pain in his eyes seemed to

pierce her. "I don't understand," she said, forcing herself not to reach out to him.

"How could you?" He threw his arms into the air. "This must have been like growing up in a damned Norman Rockwell painting."

Her heart ached as the meaning of his words sank in. "I suppose it was."

He laughed. "But I'll bet you're thinking that every family has their problems, right?" A bitter laugh escaped him. "I keep thinking that if we'd ever stayed in one place long enough, my father might have noticed how many vodka bottles my mother fed the trash can. Maybe then he could have saved her."

Lauren ached to take his hand. She hadn't understood the depth of his pain until that moment. "How hard for you both."

He turned his back to her. "My father remarried within the year. I get an occasional change of address card from him."

Lauren felt welded to the floor, wanting to reach out to him, but knowing she needed to wait, to listen.

When he turned to her again, determination had replaced the pain. "Last year I learned some hard lessons about taking risks, about toeing the line to protect people you care about. And believe me, Lauren, if I'd turned the coin in, someone I care about would have been hurt."

She felt a new surge of pain at his words. "A woman?" she asked.

He looked genuinely taken aback. "No, someone that I work with at the university named Luke Ebsin." A look of regret altered his expression. "Coosa ruined his reputation. Luke is my mentor, like a father to me. It almost killed him, and I was to blame."

Lauren struggled to make sense of what he was saying. "I don't understand. What is Coosa?"

He frowned. "You know about the Coosa excavation, Lauren. Why else would you have picked the coin?"

Her head throbbed with frustration, and she felt a tear slide down her cheek. She looked deep into his eyes, willing him to believe her. "For the last time, I didn't plant the coin. And I don't know about Coosa."

Jesse held her gaze, the silence growing between them. Finally he sighed. "Luke spent his career—his life—trying to trace the steps of the early Spanish explorers. Using Luke's research, I was certain that we'd located one of the chiefdoms that they occupied. I wanted him to see his dream come true before he retired. But . . . the excavation was a bad decision."

"It wasn't the right location?"

His expression told her that Jesse was still struggling to believe that she didn't know about the excavation. He shook his head. "No, it wasn't. And the disappointment, the criticism, and the bad press that the university received took its toll on Luke. From that point on I vowed to make things as easy as possible for him."

Lauren nodded. "You vowed not to take any chances?"

"Right. At least until Luke retired. You have to understand, Lauren. My job—the people I work with—that's the only thing that's ever been there for me." He cupped her face in his hands. "At least until you."

She felt her resolve falter at his words, felt her anger melting under the shining warmth of his eyes.

"That's why I didn't tell you, even though you deserved to know the truth."

"But why the ruse to begin with, Jesse?"

"That wasn't my decision. The other route is by far the better choice for the interstate, but if it looked like the highway department hadn't considered the two equally, they would have had an angry mob of locals to contend with."

Looking up into his eyes, she wanted to believe him. It would be easier on her ego and her heart, but she wasn't ready to be that vulnerable again.

"You don't believe me, do you?" he asked.

She shook her head and pulled her gaze from his, staring at the floor instead. "Maybe."

He slid his hands down her neck, tangling them in her hair. "I should have trusted you. I should have told you the truth." One hand played against her jaw, and his thumb began to caress her lower lip.

She caught his wrist, stopping the distracting teasing. Her best defense was her anger, so she summoned it like an old friend. "You lied to me because you were in too deep. That much I understand. So what's your excuse for making love to me?"

He pulled her to him, pressing the palm of her hand against his chest, just over his heart. His hand tightened on hers when she would have pulled away. "I made love to you because I love you."

The beat of his heart ticked off the seconds as she stared at him.

He was only saying what she wanted to hear. Or maybe it was a last-ditch effort to gain her trust. Could the coin, or maybe the excavation site itself, be worth that much? A voice inside her, a small and bitter voice, said not to believe him. But her heart ached for what could be, and told her to take the chance that he truly loved her.

For better or for worse, she listened.

Lauren withdrew her hand and laid her cheek against his chest, feeling the even rhythm of his heartbeat. "Please don't be lying," she whispered.

He drew her head up to look at him. "I'm not lying," he said. He looked at the ceiling. "It scares me to death." He laughed softly, his single dimple showing as he grinned down at her again. "But I love you, Lauren Adams."

Some elemental part of her responded to the truth in his words, and her anger seeped away, leaving her clinging to Jesse with a love and a hunger she'd never felt before. The heat from his body branded her through the thin shirt she wore.

He loved her.

She cut off a sob as she moved into the circle of his arms, feeding off his warmth, allowing herself to believe the words, one by one.

He backed her into her bedroom and closed the door, then she heard him groan as he molded her body against his, the deep rumble vibrating from his chest and into hers. A ripple of passion ran through her, drawing her nipples into tight buds. As if he sensed the change, Jesse's hands were suddenly beneath her shirt, sliding upward, warm, seeking until they reached her breasts.

He filled his hands with her, lifting her breasts while he trapped her nipples between his fingers, teasing them with gentle pressure until she felt the room begin to spin. She shut her eyes, soaring, reveling in his touch.

She ached to feel his hips against hers, but his hands

trapped between them denied her the rest of his body by a few maddening inches. She arched her back, closing the gap between their hips, and his rock-hard arousal pressed against her. Her most feminine of muscles contracted as a surge of warm, liquid desire filled her.

She pulled his shirt from the waistband of his jeans and pushed it up, eager to touch his skin, to lean her head against his chest and smell the musky, intoxicating scent that belonged only to him. He tugged the shirt from her hands and pulled it over his head in one motion, leaving his bare chest glimmering in the sunlight from the window.

She reached for the top button of his jeans, but just as she would have freed it from its buttonhole, she felt the pressure of Jesse's arms behind her knees. She was in his arms for only a few strides. Just long enough for him to deposit her on the edge of her bed.

The old oak bed was tall, and she found herself staring at his chest. She reached out, running her fingers across his tight, tanned skin. Then she leaned forward and flicked her tongue against one hardened flat nipple. Jesse gasped softly, his hands tightening on her shoulders. She planted a soft kiss in the center of his chest before pressing her tongue to his other nipple, teasing it with the warmth of her mouth.

Jesse moaned. Grasping her lightly under the chin, he tilted her head until she was looking into his eyes. Before when they'd made love, the storm had darkened the room, casting them in shadows. Today the sunlight streamed in through the window behind the bed, making her feel warm and alive.

As she looked into his amber-brown eyes, glowing with desire, she knew there was something else there. *It's love*, she thought, finally believing it. And she knew he saw it was mirrored in her eyes as well.

No matter what, even if he left tomorrow, her heart would always belong to this man. No piece of paper, no vows spoken aloud for the benefit of others, could ever bind her more solidly than giving herself to him today.

She touched the side of his face. "I love you, too, Jesse McCain," she said, her voice even and sure.

He bent to kiss her, his lips soft against hers before his tongue slipped between them, seeking hers with a possessiveness that hadn't been there before. When he pulled away, she lay back on the bed, her eyes inviting him to follow.

He unfastened his jeans and, with frustrating slowness, pushed them over his hips, taking his briefs with them. Lauren stared. Even if she'd tried, she couldn't have imagined the perfection of the raw, masculine beauty that stood before her. Illuminated by the sunlight, dust motes swirled like magic powder around his broad shoulders, falling in a tantalizing dance toward his hips. Drawing her gaze down to his arousal.

The silence of the old house and the golden sunlight that enveloped them made what was happening seem imaginary. As if in a dream, she reached out to caress him. She heard his sharp intake of breath as her fingers closed around his velvety hardness.

"I need you," he said. A muscle in his jaw jumped as he grasped her hips, pulling her toward the edge of the mattress. One hand lingered beneath her buttocks while the other circled around her hand that held him. Together they guided him into her.

Lauren had never felt so completely filled up. With love and with the thick, pulsing ecstasy of Jesse's arousal.

She smiled a secret smile, pleased that she was the reason he was so hard and ready within her. She opened her eyes. Jesse was still standing, his face registering a mix of ecstasy and pain born of restraint. A vein on the side of his temple pulsed, and Lauren thought for a brief moment that she saw tears in his eyes.

Wrapping her legs around his hips, she pulled him deep within her, her upper body arching against his chest as she did. He grabbed her by the shoulders and lifted the worn T-shirt over her head, tossing it behind him. Wrapping his fingers behind her neck, he kissed her, his tongue mimicking each thrust of his hips. She moaned against his mouth, already incredibly near release.

Reaching up, she tugged loose the rubber band that bound his hair, before falling back against the mattress. The dark hair fell about his face and shoulders, giving him an untamed look. It was fitting. What was happening between them was as old and primitive as life itself. It was as if, by freeing his hair, she had released a tidal wave of passion. He thrust deeper into her, rhythmic and hard.

Lauren wanted it to go on forever, but she was already on the brink of fulfillment. She moaned, twisting handfuls of the sheet in her fists. Jesse thrust faster, until she wasn't aware of anything but him and the friction of him moving deep inside her.

It was beyond anything she'd ever experienced before, even when they had been together the first time. This time he loved her, and she wanted him, every bit of him. She wanted to feel his seed spilling into her, even more than she needed her own release.

"Jesse, please . . ." she cried, burying the side of her face into the mattress. "I need you."

He cried out, a low, guttural sound that only heightened her own arousal. His upper body fell onto hers, his sweat-slick chest sliding against her sensitive nipples. He took one in his mouth, suckling as he thrust one final time.

He poured into her with fiery warmth, spreading inside her as he seemed to grow larger still. His pulsing orgasm was her undoing. Her muscles tightened around him, convulsing with a climax that drew him deeper inside her. He collapsed on top of her, and together they rode out the tidal wave of passion that left their breathing ragged and their bodies spent.

Jesse seemed reluctant to withdraw as he eased himself fully onto the mattress, staying buried within her as he did. He rolled her over onto her side, one leg draped over her thigh, holding her against him.

He traced his index finger lazily around the outline of her lips. "Did that erase our differences, or do I need to try again?"

She laughed, and brushed the tip of his finger with her tongue. "I was going to say yes, but since you put it like that . . ."

"Wait a minute. I thought I had a satisfied customer here," he teased.

She bit his finger. "You do. But I'm not sure I ought to let you up until I'm certain that you believe I didn't plant the coin."

"Then don't." He kissed her, his lips artfully playing over hers until her heart ached with a completeness that only he could give her.

When had she fallen so helplessly in love with him?

There was no other reason why she was willing to let the argument go unchallenged for now. She rested her head against his chest, and from the angle she was at caught sight of their reflection in her vanity mirror.

The sun streamed through the trees outside her window, casting their entwined bodies in dappled golden and green light. *It's a perfect union,* a voice in her head whispered. *Find a way to make it last.* She sleepily closed her eyes, but the image of them remained.

Lauren stirred in her sleep, wadding the expanse of sheet she held against her chest. Jesse gently withdrew his body from hers, feeling cold from the loss of her warm sheath that had held him. Her mere breathing had kept him hard inside her, and he was entertaining thoughts of waking her.

But he knew he needed to call Leo Harbison. They had left the poor man standing, looking more than a little bewildered, in the middle of the restaurant. Jesse reminded himself that since he was under contract with the highway department, Leo Harbison was technically his boss.

He pulled on his underwear and headed for the study, but remembering that Cassie and Ted could come into the house at any minute, he stopped and put on his jeans as well. He felt drugged, a wonderful, satisfying kind of lethargy, and he would have given anything to stay in bed with Lauren. He looked at her, her mouth forming a small, angelic smile while she slept.

He walked back to the bed, unable to stop himself from smoothing a wayward strand of hair that rested against the corner of her mouth. He remembered another time, when she had insisted on accompanying him on the shovel test, when his fingers had ached to be able to brush a strand of hair from her lips.

He smiled. Something had happened between them today, something he hadn't even known he wanted until that morning. Lauren might not be willing to admit the truth about the coin, but he didn't care. She'd said she loved him. And she was willing to forgive him for his lies. That was all that mattered. Their lovemaking had bridged the gap that the lies had formed, and Jesse intended to never look back.

He walked barefoot across the hardwood floor of Lauren's bedroom, closing the door gently behind him before heading down the hallway to the study. The shutters were closed, making the small room darker than the rest of the house.

He flipped on the overhead light, and the old glass dome immediately brightened the room. He took in the perfectly straight rows of books that lined the bookshelves, the paisley balloon valances that topped each window. Lauren's desk was positioned at a fashionable angle in a corner of the room, with a curious-looking old brass container sitting in the center of it.

He walked toward it, thinking the beat-up old bucket looked familiar. When he sat down in the desk chair to get a better look, the first thing he noticed was a large yellow note stuck to the side. In almost illegible handwriting it read: I told you they were in the attic. P.S. What was with the paper clips?—Cassie.

Jesse looked at Lauren's appointment book, now neatly closed beside the bowl of paper clips, and remembered that he'd accidentally knocked the bowl over when he'd discovered her appointment with Leo. He peered over the side of the brass container and found it filled to the brim with arrowheads and spear points. So Lauren hadn't given up on finding them after all.

He lifted one perfect specimen, running his thumb over the delicate-looking flint. It was charcoal-black, with a ridge of creamy white bordering the base. It was exquisite workmanship, obviously intended for ceremonial use, and incredibly had survived the centuries without a mar. He turned it over, surprised to see a tiny piece of white paper taped to the underside. He squinted to make out the faded, somewhat shaky handwriting. "Found by Lauren in the strawberry patch, May 1975," he read aloud. People rarely cataloged the location of their finds, rendering them almost useless from a professional viewpoint. Excited, Jesse picked up another arrowhead. Even though this one was not a near-perfect specimen, someone had meticulously labeled it as well. It read: Found by Thomas—digging the irrigation pond, April 1962.

One by one he removed the artifacts, and found each had been loyally labeled, by Lauren's grandmother if his suspicions were correct. He started to replace the arrowheads when something about the container began nagging him again. It *was* familiar. He ran his thumb across the rim, mulling over the possibilities.

Then it hit him.

Holding the old container up to the light, he examined the rough, dented brass from all angles. With its slightly flared bottom and rolled rim, he was surprised it hadn't occurred to him earlier. It exactly matched a candlestick found at an excavation site he'd worked in south Alabama.

A sixteenth-century Spanish candlestick.

With shaking hands, he turned the container upside down. Sure enough, a small scrap of paper was taped to the bottom. He read aloud, "Found by Cassandra—by the willow tree at the creek, August 1977."

The willow tree at the creek . . . He remembered standing by a willow tree watching Lauren, her long legs stretched in front of her as the creek rolled over them, the crystal-clear water parting at her waist. He shook his head. He'd actually convinced himself that it had all been a seduction routine, that she'd only pretended to find the coin.

Instead, she had been telling the truth all along. He cringed as he thought of the harsh accusations he'd thrown at her. She loved him, had made love with him even though he'd refused to believe her. Jesse ran his hand through his hair. He didn't deserve her.

Another revelation hit him. He'd thought holding the rifle on him had only been part of her act, but she had truly suspected him of trying to steal the coin. His eyebrows shot up in delayed alarm. Hell, if he'd known she was serious, he wouldn't have been so arrogant.

He massaged his forehead, thinking of the angel asleep in the other room. The innocent look was definitely deceiving. Lauren was one woman who knew how to take care of herself. In fact, if not for him she would probably have everything under control by now. No doubt about it, Lauren would have been better off without him.

Maybe making love to her had been a mistake. His fingers stilled. In a funny way, things had been less real to him when he'd thought Lauren had deceived him. Now he understood just how much she trusted him.

He hoped that trust would last.

He picked up the receiver of Lauren's desk phone and punched out Ken's work number as he ran his hand through his disheveled hair, anxious for his friend to pick up the phone.

"Lab," Ken finally answered, sounding distracted.

"What did I interrupt?" Jesse asked.

"Hey, Jess." There was a rattling noise as Ken obviously shifted the receiver to his other ear. "I thought you'd still be in bed after tying one on last night."

"Well . . ." Jesse hesitated, thinking he had, in fact, been in bed until a few minutes ago. But what he'd discovered in those few minutes made it seem like hours since he'd left Lauren's bedroom. "I need you to do me a favor."

"It's done. Whatcha need?" Ken asked with his usual good-natured willingness.

"Set up a meeting with the Early Exploration Commission members, and call Leo Harbison and ask him to meet us at the university."

"Okay, I guess." Ken sounded unsure. "For when?"

Jesse looked at his watch, calculating the long drive to the university. "Four o'clock this afternoon."

"What?" Jesse wasn't surprised that Ken sounded stunned. Summoning the members of the commission on such short notice meant interrupting more than a few busy professors and professional historians. Not an enviable task. "What for?"

"It's a surprise," Jesse said.

"You want me to call twenty-one of the most prominent people I know and tell them to drop what they're doing because Jesse McCain has a surprise for them?"

"Yes."

———❖———❖———

Lauren cracked one eye, instinctively aware that someone was standing over her.

Expecting to find Jesse, she was disappointed to see Cassie instead. Her sister's hands were propped on her blue-jean-clad hips, and her brightly painted lips were curled into a definite smirk.

"A little afternoon delight, huh?" Cassie asked.

Lauren moaned, pulling the sheet over her head.

Cassie jerked it back down, the unmistakable aroma of horse sweat wafting through the air as she did. "You're not getting out of this one that easy," she said.

"Yeah, and you need a shower."

"And you look like you need an oxygen mask," Cassie retorted. She waved her hand through the air. "Look at this place."

Lauren's usually perfectly made bed was in shambles, and her T-shirt and panties were lying in a heap on the floor.

Cassie walked to the bedroom door, retrieving the cover of the phone book with Lauren's note scrawled across the back.

"Sister sleeping," she read aloud. "Good grief!" She tossed it in the air. "Couldn't you come up with something better than that?"

"That was . . . before," Lauren sputtered.

"I thought you were mad at Bones, anyway. What gives?"

Lauren smiled a Cheshire cat smile. "I'm not mad at him anymore."

Cassie laughed. "Well, I'm confused, but I've been telling you for months now that what you needed to

improve your sour attitude was a good roll in the hay."
She picked up Lauren's T-shirt and tossed it to her. "By
the way, Bones came down to the barn about thirty minutes ago and said to tell you he'd call you soon."

"He left without saying good-bye?" Lauren asked,
disappointed.

"Yeah, but if it's any consolation, he had the same
lovesick-cow expression on his face that you do."

"The cow comment aside, it is a consolation. Did he
say where he was going?"

"No," Cassie answered. "But he roared out of here
on two wheels."

A crashing sound echoed down the hall, coming
from the kitchen below.

"Sorry," a masculine voice called. "Nothing's broken."

Cassie looked suddenly uncomfortable. "I hope you
don't mind. I invited Ted in for a late lunch. We've been
working the horse off and on all morning and—"

Lauren threw a pillow at Cassie, interrupting her. "I
thought wounded men weren't your cup of tea."

"Nothing's going on, honestly. But he's a really nice
guy, and I thought that we should get to know each
other since I'm going to be working with Alyssa."

Lauren's eyes went round with astonishment. "You
agreed to work with Ted's daughter?" She forced her
voice to a calmer tone, not wanting to spook Cassie away
from something she knew would be good for her. "I
thought you didn't want to."

Cassie sank down on the edge of the bed. "I haven't
met her yet, but Ted's told me what an incredible kid she
is. You wouldn't believe what she's been through in the
last year and a half."

Lauren pulled the sheet over one shoulder, toga style, and sat up. Reaching out with her free hand, she tugged her sister's shirtsleeve. "I'm proud of you."

Cassie only shrugged, brushing imaginary lint from Lauren's comforter. Another crash sounded from downstairs.

Lauren laughed. "You'd better go down. It sounds like he could use your help."

"See you in a minute?" Cassie asked.

Lauren nodded. "Yeah. I'm just going to shower first." As Cassie left, Lauren called to her. "Hey, how about making me one of whatever you're about to eat? I'm starved."

Cassie winked at her, tapping her still-perfect red fingernails against the doorframe. "It'll do it to you every time."

Lauren didn't linger under the refreshingly tepid spray of the showerhead. Instead she rushed, feeling more energetic than she had in a long time, and eager to get the north pasture mowed before nightfall.

After a quick drying off, she slipped into a worn pair of jeans and a T-shirt, and fished around in her closet until she emerged wearing a black-and-green baseball cap with a tractor company's insignia on the front. Once she'd tugged on her work boots and looked in the mirror, she hoped Jesse didn't make any surprise appearances that afternoon.

As much as she wanted to see him again, she doubted either of them was ready for her in such a getup.

A shifting noise caught her attention, and she was surprised to find that Cassie had set a glass of iced tea and a ham and cheese sandwich on her vanity. She devoured the meal and was bounding down the stairs in no time. When she leaned around the corner of the kitchen to thank Cassie, she gaped at the scene that greeted her. Ted Clarke's arms were wrapped around her sister, his mouth on hers in a passionate kiss. Cassie was arched back over the kitchen sink, holding a plate in one hand and a dish towel in the other. Lauren ducked back around the corner, suffocating the gasp that threatened to give her away.

Something was definitely wrong with that picture. Then it occurred to her. Judging from Cassie's posture, she'd been caught off guard. That was something that rarely, if ever, happened. Lauren smiled, thinking her sister might have finally met her match.

She tiptoed, or came as close to it as she could in work boots, across the foyer and slipped out the front door.

The tractor started on the first try. That was a good omen, she thought, as she put it in first gear and bumped along the gravel road that led to the north pasture.

As she began the monotonous, back and forth mowing pattern, her mind drifted. Naturally, her thoughts were of Jesse. She pulled off the baseball cap and wrapped her hair in a twist before socking the cap back on. The wind played against her moist neck, reminding her of the sweet kisses Jesse had planted there. She felt her body react to the memory. Maybe she wouldn't be so sorry if he caught her in this ridiculous-looking outfit, after all, she thought, stealing a glance at the road.

He'd said he loved her, but he hadn't said anything about being with her permanently. And suddenly, she couldn't imagine it any other way. She looked around the valley, thinking how much her home meant to her. Tears came to her eyes as she pictured her grandparents carving the old home place out of the thick woods with sheer determination; the lazy summer days she and Cassie had spent under their roof and their loving protection.

Yet when she considered Jesse, he put her ties to her family in perspective. She loved him and she always would. And maybe she could learn to love the nomadic life he led. She smiled. She knew she could, as long as she was in his arms each night.

Cassie would think she'd lost her mind, but as soon as they were alone, Lauren would ask her about putting the farm up for sale.

"Lauren!" Cassie's voice broke into her thoughts, her call barely rising above the noise of the tractor.

Lauren waved, signaling that she'd heard, and headed toward her.

"What's up?" she asked after stopping the tractor in front of the house.

Cassie stood on the front stoop, barefoot, her cheeks rosily flushed. "Ted wanted to give you this month's board money," she said.

Lauren nodded, swinging one leg over the elevated seat of the old tractor. "I'll come in and write him a receipt," she said. She jumped down, her legs shaky from the constant vibration of the tractor.

"Hi, Ted," she called as she entered the kitchen. She wondered if it was only her imagination that he looked a bit sheepish.

"Hey there," he said in his heavy Southern drawl, glancing down at his feet. "I'm sorry you had to stop what you were doing."

What had happened to the confident businessman she'd met a few days ago? she wondered. As his light blue eyes met hers, it dawned on her that what was happening between him and Cassie was as much a surprise to Ted as it had been to her sister. He probably hadn't dated since his wife died.

"That's okay," she said, massaging her thighs. "You probably saved me from a midnight charley horse."

"Here's your first month's board." He handed her a check. "And here's my business card in case there's anything you need."

She accepted the card, scanning it. "You're a builder," she commented. "Did Cassie tell you she's a real estate agent?"

"Yeah, she did," Ted said with a shy grin. "Your sister is quite a gal."

Lauren couldn't help but blush at his country forthrightness. It had probably sealed quite a few business deals for him. People in these parts appreciated that type of honesty, not a slick, rehearsed come-on. And apparently it had worked on Cassie too.

Lauren spotted her purse, still lying on the kitchen table where she'd slung it earlier. Was it only a few hours ago that she had wanted never to see Jesse again? She grabbed the purse before she headed up the stairs to her study, tucking the check in her billfold as she went.

"I'll only be a minute," she called over her shoulder. "I want to write you a receipt."

As she sat down at her desk, her elbow brushed something gritty. She swept it away and reached for her new receipt book, a victorious excitement uncurling in her stomach. Her first boarder. She could only hope that once word got out, Ted would be the first of many.

She heard Cassie giggle downstairs, then Ted's deep

laughter. She shook her head. This day was turning out all right after all.

"Hey, Sis," Cassie called, her voice echoing down the hall. "Did you see the arrowheads?"

"You found them?" Excited, Lauren glanced around her. "Where did you put them?"

"In the middle of your desk, silly," Cassie answered.

Lauren looked down at the ring of dirt in the middle of her desk. Swallowing her panic, she jerked her purse into her lap, burrowing through its contents as her head began to throb.

"Oh, Jesse, you didn't," she cried as her hand pulled out an empty square of black felt.

TEN

Lauren sat at the desk, her forehead cradled in her hands. Why had she let her guard down? The words "I love you" were so simple to say. What had made her believe him? *Because you wanted to*, a voice whispered in her head.

She bit her lip in an effort not to cry. It just didn't make sense. She understood why Jesse wanted the coin, but arrowheads were easy to come by. Ask any local farmer, and he would pull out a boxful. Yet the loss of the arrowheads was what hurt the most.

There were decades' worth of memories tied up in those simple artifacts. When she was a child, the thrill of finding one had been only slightly more exciting than the trip she and her grandmother would make to the library to look up its origin and date. In the spring when her grandfather tilled the garden, she and her cousins would compete to see who could find the most arrowheads. Lauren smiled a sad smile. She'd always won.

Maybe, she thought, there was a reasonable explanation for what Jesse had done. After all, he had told Cassie he'd call. A rush of cynicism stiffened her back. What was she trying to do to herself? That was the oldest line in the book. She'd been a fool twice now, and she didn't intend to go for a triple.

But what could she do? The thought of calling Leo Harbison made her blood run cold. It was clear he and Jesse had a good working relationship, if not friendship, and he probably thought she was a true crackpot by now. Asking about a coin that was, at least in his mind, nonexistent, and canceling a lunch appointment on the spot. No, there had to be some other way to prove Jesse had taken the artifacts.

In a rush of excitement, she buried her hand back into her purse, her short-clipped fingernails scraping against the lint and grit in the bottom until her fingers closed around the key to her dilemma: The key to Jesse's apartment.

"Yes," she whispered aloud.

She quickly wrote out a receipt for Ted and whisked the paper from her receipt book. She didn't want Ted and Cassie to know anything was wrong. The last thing she wanted was to answer a truckload of questions and, if she was honest with herself, to let her sister know what a fool she'd been.

As she headed out of the study, she caught a glimpse of her reflection in the bookcase glass. Yikes, she thought. Not only did she look ridiculous, she was bound to call attention to herself in the Farmer Brown getup. She ducked into her dressing room and kicked off the jeans and work boots, then let the baseball cap and dirty T-shirt join them in a heap at her feet.

She got some perverse satisfaction in choosing a sleeveless black turtleneck that clung to her like a second skin, and a tight-fitting pair of black jeans. Now this outfit, she thought, was just right for breaking in to someone's apartment. Besides, she looked good in it, and that gave her confidence. Lord knows, she needed every bit of nerve she could find.

Finally she brushed out her hair, caught it in a silver clip at the base of her neck, then lightly sprayed her wrists with perfume to cover the gas-engine smell that lingered from the tractor. She might run into a neighbor, or even Jesse, and she didn't want to arouse any suspicion.

Cassie and Ted looked a little bewildered when she reemerged in the drastically different outfit. Cassie's hand rested on a deflated-looking lemon that had fast been on its way to becoming lemonade, but she didn't say anything.

Wait a minute, Lauren thought. Cassie was making fresh lemonade—and she was at a loss for words? Good grief, her sister had it bad.

Lauren slid the receipt across the kitchen table. "Thanks, Ted. You don't know how much this means to me right now."

He nodded, and Cassie looked as if she were about to burst from curiosity. Lauren never could hide anything from her sister, but thankfully, she didn't ask any questions.

"I'll be out for a while," she called over her shoulder as she hightailed it around the corner of the kitchen. "Lock up when you leave."

As soon as she was outside, away from her sister's probing stare, she felt her confidence rise. She slid behind the wheel of her car and switched the wiper blades on, watching them cut a path through the dirt and grit that the tractor had stirred up. She could do this, she thought. Jesse had taken some important things of hers, and she intended to get them back.

As she turned onto the main road, she held down the button that opened the sunroof and turned up the classic rock song on the radio. She refused to acknowledge the painful ache in her chest. Once she had the coin and arrowheads back, she would be able to come to terms with the fact that Jesse had betrayed her. Until then, she refused to think about it.

Right now she needed to concentrate on forming a plan.

However, when Lauren pulled into the spacious parking lot of Jesse's apartment complex, she still didn't have a plan. At least she didn't see Jesse's Jeep anywhere. It was almost completely dark, but the streetlamps cast their bluish light, effectively illuminating the parking lot.

Her heart pounding in her chest, she walked up to the door of his apartment. She cocked her head, allowing herself a few seconds to listen for any activity inside before she slid the key into the lock. All she heard was the soft hum of the air-conditioning unit. She turned the key and pushed the door open.

She was met with only the eerie silence of an empty apartment.

Once inside, Lauren pressed her back against the door and drew in several deep, calming breaths before she found the nerve to glance around the apartment.

It was messier than it had been before. She poked her head into the tiny kitchen area, noticing an open bread sack lying on the kitchen counter. Beside it, the coffeemaker flashed a red warning light, signaling that the automatic shutoff had been activated.

Maybe he'd been in such a hurry to interrupt her meeting with Leo Harbison that morning that he'd forgotten to shut it off. Serves him right, she thought. But her stomach gave a painful twist at the thought of the apartment catching fire, and she switched the power button to the off position.

After that, she began a methodical search of the apartment, flipping on as few lights as possible at a time, her eyes scanning the tops of every flat surface. The kitchen and the living room turned up nothing. She checked each corner of the apartment, but found only stacks of excavation reports and volumes of research books. It still surprised her that someone this dedicated to his work would stoop so low as to steal artifacts.

So far, she had avoided going into Jesse's bedroom, recalling the way her emotions had surfaced the last time she'd ventured into that personal territory. But she'd checked out all the other possibilities.

Lauren took a deep breath, determined to put her wounded heart on hold long enough to finish what she'd started. But as her gaze took in the unmade bed, a sick feeling settled in the pit of her stomach.

From somewhere behind her a key rattled, and her heart turned over in her chest.

Jesse!

She poked her head out the bedroom door to make a quick survey of the living room, relieved that she'd turned off all the lights but the single lamp that had been on already. Thankfully, the bedroom door had originally been closed, so she pushed it to behind her—just before the front door's hinges creaked and she heard heavy footsteps on the threshold.

"I thought I had locked it." Jesse's voice sounded

even deeper in the sparsely furnished apartment. She heard keys jingle again, and a dead bolt being slid into place.

Lauren looked around her, willing herself not to panic. The overhead light! She hit the switch, and felt as if her heart would beat right out of her chest. This was it. Surely they had seen the light go out and would come after her at any minute. But as her eyes adjusted to the dark and no one burst through the door, her heartbeat settled into a more normal rhythm.

"I must have been in such a hurry to get to Lauren's, that I didn't lock the door," Jesse said casually. "And then, of course, I had to rush on to Birmingham to keep her from meeting with Leo. Come on in."

Damn him. It was his fault she was cowering in the dark, feeling like the criminal *he* was. Soon, she could make out the shadowy figures of the furniture in the small bedroom. When she noticed the hazy blue light from the streetlamps peeking through an oversize curtain near the bed, she sighed with relief. It had to be a sliding glass door. She inched toward it, carefully feeling her way in the dark.

She pushed the thick curtain to one side, and her hand brushed the wooden handle of a sliding glass door. Inching her fingers down the handle, she finally touched the locking mechanism and pushed it down. The lock gave a hard click, and she flattened herself against the floor, waiting to see if anyone would investigate.

All she heard was a shuffling sound and the crinkling noise of a paper sack. "Ken?" Jesse called, seemingly from the kitchen.

"Yo?" The gruff voice Lauren recognized from the Green Shamrock sounded much nearer.

"You want a beer?"

"Definitely. I think we should celebrate, my friend."

Lauren heard the unmistakable sound of two beer cans being opened. She prayed they would switch on the television or the radio, then she would try to slide the door open and make her escape.

"So you're celebrating getting rid of me, huh? Some friend." Jesse's voice sounded light, jovial, while Lauren stopped breathing.

He was leaving? Her chest ached so hard, she pressed her fist against it.

"Ah, you know I'll miss you," Ken answered. "But when good fortune falls into your lap, you'd better not ask questions."

"I'll drink to that," Jesse answered.

Lauren balled her hands into fists. She didn't know how much more she could take. They were actually celebrating stealing from her. The coin must have been worth more than she'd dreamed, and he'd sold it. She couldn't think of any other reason he would suddenly be able to leave his job.

"Where will you live?" Ken asked.

"I'm not sure yet," Jesse answered. "But I'm sure as hell not staying here."

His words echoed in her head. He wasn't just leaving his job, he was leaving town. And leaving her.

What else had she imagined? That he would call, saying the coin was worth a million dollars—and that he had sold it so that they could drive off into the sunset together? In real life there were no perfect sunsets, no happy endings.

She had to get out of the apartment. She pushed the aluminum frame that held the heavy glass, suddenly not caring whether she was heard or not. Instead of giving her away, the door slid smoothly on its track, letting in a cool evening breeze.

Forget lying in the dark, hiding like some night animal afraid to come out of its hole, she thought. If this was what loving someone reduced her to, then she didn't need it. Forget Jesse McCain. He could do what he wanted with the artifacts, but he'd taken the last piece of her heart.

She stood and slipped through the small opening, silently closed the door behind her, and disappeared like a cat over the side of the patio fence.

"You're saying the rumor is true then, Mr. Harbison?" Lauren asked. "Yes, yes. I understand." She leaned back in the kitchen chair and grimaced at the ceiling. "No, I didn't hear it from you."

Her hand was trembling as she hung up the phone. The first thing she'd had to do that morning was to confirm that the alternate interstate route had been picked. At least Jesse hadn't lied to her about that. Her heart gave a funny tilt. She'd believed him with the strength of her very soul when he'd told her he loved her. She shook her head. Maybe part of her still did.

Dangerous thoughts, Lauren, her mind scolded. She'd escaped Jesse's betrayal with her sanity, if not her heart, intact. Now she needed to get on with her life.

She started by making a list of things to do, certain that by the time she finished, loving Jesse McCain would be the furthest thing from her mind. Alyssa's horse needed to be reshod, and Lauren had promised Ted she'd meet the blacksmith. Then she needed to pick up a salt block and grain from the feed store, finish mowing the north pasture, and order paint for the outside of the barn. A load of shavings was to be delivered that afternoon by five o'clock. She sighed. And she needed groceries.

She picked up a pencil, scrawled the word "groceries" across the top of her notebook, then neatly numbered each line. But she could only think of one thing she needed. Pistachio ice cream.

By the next day, Lauren had scratched all the things off her list, and her chest still ached every time she thought of Jesse. And that was more often than she cared to admit, even to herself. Instead of forgetting him, she'd only succeeded in exhausting herself.

She was sitting at the kitchen table, eating a bowl of pistachio ice cream, complete with pistachio nuts sprinkled on top, when Cassie burst through the front door.

"Anyone home?" Cassie didn't bother to wait for an answer as she trotted into the kitchen, coming to a dead stop in front of Lauren. She put her hand over her heart in mock distress. "What are you doing?"

Lauren shrugged and plopped a huge spoonful of ice cream in her mouth. "Taking a break and mail-order shopping," she said through cold lips.

"Wait, let me sit down." Cassie pretended to stagger toward a chair. "You're taking a break in the middle of the day?"

Lauren shoved her completed list toward her sister. "Read it and weep," she said.

"Good grief," Cassie said, her eyes round as she read the list. "What are you trying to do, kill yourself?"

Lauren only responded by spooning another mound of ice cream into her mouth.

"So what are you shopping for?" Cassie asked.

Lauren thumped the thin page of the catalog. "I'm thinking about getting a television."

Cassie looked around her. "You don't . . ." She looked around again. "You don't have a TV? How could I have never noticed that?" Her voice grew louder. "Why on earth don't you have a TV?"

"I let mine go with the apartment when I moved. I was so sick of people that I didn't want anyone around, even if they were only on television." She shrugged. "But last night I was thinking I might like to have one."

"Something's up with Jesse, isn't it?" Cassie asked.

The fact that her sister had actually called him by his name made Lauren realize Cassie was on to her. There was little hope of blowing the situation off, so she opted for the truth and looked her sister straight in the eye.

"Jesse stole Grandmother's arrowheads and the coin. He never loved me, and he's never coming back." She blurted the words out all at once, afraid she'd buckle under the pain if she had to explain in slow, agonizing detail.

An odd expression crossed Cassie's face before she lunged for the cordless phone. She shoved it under Lauren's nose. "Call the police."

"No—"

"Call the police."

Lauren shook her head, overwhelmed by the barrage of emotions that were assaulting her.

"Okay, Lauren, either you call them right this minute or I will." Cassie began to punch the buttons.

Lauren stood and snatched the phone from her sister's hand. "You don't understand, I don't—"

"You don't what, Lauren?"

"I don't believe he did it."

A devious smile crossed Cassie's face. "Neither do I," she said calmly.

It didn't take long for Lauren to understand Cassie's ruse. Her hands still trembled, and her pulse was still pounding, but she couldn't be angry with her sister. "You're like Sigmund Freud on caffeine."

Cassie hugged her, squeezing her shoulders so hard and releasing her so quickly that Lauren almost dropped the phone. "So why pay for years of therapy when you have me?"

"I can think of so many reasons, one of which is that I want to strangle you right now."

"A fool could tell by looking at you that you're still in love with the man. And if I know you, that means you don't believe he could betray you. You just needed to admit it to yourself, that's all."

Lauren felt a cloud of fear extinguish the spark of new hope she felt. "Now all Jesse has to do is prove me right."

Cassie headed toward the door. "You've got great instincts, Lauren. You just switched them off a long time ago when it comes to men. Even if Jesse proves you wrong, you still win."

"How's that?"

Cassie drummed a cadence on the doorframe with her fingernails. "Because you had to learn to trust again sometime."

Lauren looked at her sister with new understanding. When had she gone from being the little imp who constantly antagonized her to a grown woman capable of giving her much-needed advice?

Cassie glanced at her watch. "I'm going to start working the horse in a minute, and Ted is coming over about three o'clock this afternoon, so you won't be lonely."

Lauren opened her mouth to argue that she wasn't lonely, but Cassie held up her hands in defense.

"Hey, as soon as your television comes in, we're out of here," she said, winking.

Lauren smiled at her sister, hoping the small surge of envy she experienced didn't show. How ironic that Cassie, who had always run from anything remotely permanent, had fallen for someone with obviously strong ties to family, to the community.

And when something permanent was all Lauren had ever wanted from Jesse, she had nothing to show for her love except twisted emotions and an empty bed.

"Thanks," she said, carrying her bowl to the sink. "I'll walk out with you. I was about to take a look at the irrigation pump anyway."

Cassie gave her a sideways glance. "No offense, but I'm relieved. I was hoping that outfit wasn't just to impress the neighbors." She nodded toward Lauren's old cutoff shorts and tank top.

"What neighbors?" Lauren asked as she shoved her sister out the front door.

Cassie laughed. "Good point."

Once at the barn, Lauren leaned over the paddock fence to give Alyssa's horse a thorough ear scratching, despite Lucky's attempts to win her attention by jumping against her leg.

"Hey," she whispered, blowing softly into his velvety

nose. "Don't get too used to Cassie. She's temporary, you know. I'm the one who's going to be feeding you every day."

The little gelding only stomped his hoof and snorted, covering Lauren's pink tank top with grass-green flecks of horse slobber.

"Thanks a lot," she said, playfully tugging on his forelock.

"That serves you right for trying to get him to choose between us," Cassie said, arriving from the barn to slip the halter over the horse's head.

"With the way my luck's been running with men, I wouldn't have the nerve to try," Lauren said. Even she recognized the depressed, monotone ring to her voice, and wasn't surprised to see the look of sympathy on Cassie's face.

"It's not over yet."

"No." She shook her head, not trusting the dam of composure that held her emotions in check. She smiled a tight-lipped smile before heading inside the barn to get her equipment.

To reach to the water pump, Lauren had to drain the irrigation pond. And because it hadn't been flushed since the previous summer, she was dreading the messy, smelly task. She knew from experience that once the water was drained, she'd be met with knee-deep silt and goo, not to mention the unrecognizable bugs and reptiles that would be slithering on the concrete bottom of the man-made pond.

She unscrewed the plug on the outside of the retaining wall, and the water began rushing from the pond. Balancing her bottom on the narrow wall of the reservoir, she watched the hypnotic motion of the water being sucked out.

Cassie was right. She still loved Jesse, still believed in her heart that he wasn't capable of such betrayal. But every agonizing minute that ticked by was a countdown to the crushing pain she would feel if he failed her after all. But even when the ugly voice of doubt insisted that she'd been used, her heart still whispered, "Not Jesse. Not this time."

The hum of Ted's Cadillac barely penetrated the noise of the rushing water. He raised his hand in greeting, but headed straight for the barn—and Cassie. Tears stung the back of Lauren's eyes, but it was more a mix of happiness for her sister and self-pity than petty jealousy.

A rude, sucking noise brought her attention back to matters at hand. The level in the pond had dropped down to the thicker, murkier water that only hinted at things to come. Considerably worse things to come, she thought.

She walked to the front of the pond where her boots lay. After kicking off her tennis shoes, she pulled the thigh-high rubber boots into place, grabbed a square-edged shovel and her gloves, and eased herself into the goo.

Her boots made a squishy noise as she walked toward the overspill and began throwing shovelfuls of the heavy muck over the chest-high wall of the reservoir. Soon she was dripping in sweat and drowning in memories.

I had to rush on to Birmingham to keep Lauren from meeting with Leo, Jesse's voice echoed in her head. She threw another shovelful of silt over the wall.

"No, Jesse. I love you," she said aloud.

She began shoveling again, increasing her speed. *I'm*

sure as hell not staying here. The shovel's edge abruptly scraped the bottom of the pond as the voice of doubt returned to taunt her.

She shook her head. "You wouldn't leave me." This time she almost shouted, raising her voice so that she could hear it over the rushing water.

She mopped beads of sweat from her forehead and leaned into the handle of the shovel. The charcoal-black silt was only ankle-high now, and somewhere during the effort, Lauren had tapped into the strength of her love for Jesse. It was possible—probable even—that she would pay the price of loving him with her heart. But the funny thing was, that was okay. She believed in him.

The afternoon heat stagnated in the concrete enclosure, and the fishy smell from the bottom of the pond was overwhelming. Lauren tried to wipe a bead of sweat from her nose, but only succeeded in covering it with mud from her glove. She almost laughed out loud, feeling giddy with relief. Whatever the future brought, she could handle it, but she could no longer deny loving Jesse McCain.

A deep rumble and the sound of Lucky barking made her look up. A navy-blue car was pulling down the driveway. With its plain hubcapped wheels and square fenders, her first thought was that it was government-issue. She felt a little nervous as a second car, identical in description, followed it.

Shielding her eyes against the sun, she shifted to get a better look as the cars followed each other down the gravel road. Then she looked down at herself, at her tank top with its flecks of horse slobber and mud. Not just mud, she corrected herself—bottom-of-the-pond mud.

She looked and smelled like the creature from the black lagoon.

The cars finally stopped several yards from the irrigation pond, and she could do little else but wait until someone made an appearance. Climbing out of the goo in her rubber boots wasn't something she wanted to do in front of strangers.

The passenger door to the first car opened, and Lauren felt every muscle in her body jump at once as Jesse stepped out.

His hair was pulled back, and he wore a starched white shirt, complete with necktie. And though he also wore blue jeans and western boots, both looked new.

A second man stepped out from behind the steering wheel. He was dressed in a gray business suit and had short silver hair. Instead of acknowledging her presence, he walked over to Jesse and touched him on the arm.

Oh God, she thought. He's been arrested. The thought of Jesse, with his bond to the outdoors, to the very earth, being locked away from it . . .

The other doors to the cars opened, and six more men, dressed in similar business suits, stepped out. She smothered a gasp by pressing her lips together. Something was wrong. Terribly wrong.

At a loss as to what to do, she moved as gracefully as she could to the edge of the reservoir and leaned the shovel against the wall. She was busy removing her gloves when a familiar voice caused cold chills to run down her spine.

"Where have you been, Lauren?"

She looked up to find Jesse kneeling beside the reservoir wall, his brows knitted together in an odd expression.

Where have I been? she thought. He had disappeared two days ago and wanted to know where she'd been. She started to laugh, but couldn't seem to break the frozen expression on her face.

He reached down and touched the skin between her shoulder and her neck, and the contact sent a wonderful warmth down her arms. "I've been worried sick about you. Why haven't you answered the damn phone?"

"I . . . I've been outside a lot. I wouldn't have heard it ring."

He suddenly looked angry, and glanced at the barn. Lauren followed his gaze to Cassie, who was holding a growling Lucky at bay. "She did tell you I would call, didn't she?"

"Yes," Lauren said, a little defensively, "but—"

"But what then? Why do you look like you've just seen a ghost?"

"Why did you take the coin, Jesse?" she blurted out. "And the arrowheads?"

Before she could react, he grasped her under the arms and pulled her out of the reservoir, leaving her rubber boots stuck in the mud. He set her down on the gravel road, and she winced as the sharp rocks ground into her bare feet. She glanced at the shocked expressions on the men's faces, and quickly looked back at Jesse.

As she focused on a broad smear of goo she'd left on his white shirt, Jesse caught her chin and tipped her head until she was looking directly into his eyes. Brown, and so beautiful—they held the warmth of the earth and the fire of the sun. He took a step toward her, and she instinctively leaned into the circle of his arms.

"You thought I'd left with them?" he asked, his voice tender.

She nodded against his chest.

"Oh God, Lauren. I never meant . . ." He closed his mouth over hers, the sweet mating of their lips and the unspoken hunger as his tongue slid against hers telling her everything she needed to know.

Like a weight lifted from her shoulders, she felt the last layer of doubt melt from her heart. She clung to Jesse, never wanting to let go again.

From behind them came one tentative clapping of hands, which was soon joined by others. When Jesse finally broke their kiss, they were surrounded by seven serious-looking men in suits—all applauding.

Lauren was completely and totally embarrassed. She glanced over her shoulder to find Cassie and Ted looking on from the barn. Cassie gave her a thumbs-up sign with one hand while she held a squirming Lucky with the other. Lauren buried her face in Jesse's chest, not knowing what to do next.

"Lauren," he said, "I'd like you to meet the members of the Early Exploration Commission. Everyone, this is Lauren Adams."

Lauren could think of nothing to do except nod in their direction. "They have the artifacts?" she asked.

"You owe me a big apology," Jesse said, stretching his arms wide like a child describing the size of a fish.

"Which you will never get if you don't stop gloating."

Thankfully the sound of an approaching car—a very noisy approaching car—caused all heads to turn toward the road.

"Finally," Jesse muttered.

The car, in dire need of both a muffler and a wash, pulled to a stop behind the others. Lauren watched as Jesse's friend Ken unfolded his sizable body from the tiny old car. She felt Jesse stand a little straighter when the passenger door opened and a distinguished-looking white-haired man emerged.

Jesse squeezed her shoulder. "Now here's someone I want you to meet."

She followed his lead as he urged her forward.

Jesse clasped the older man on the shoulder affectionately. "I've been trying to reach you."

The man raised a map, smiling mischievously. "I've been busy." He turned to Lauren. "You must be Lauren Adams."

She grasped the man's outstretched hand. "Yes, I am."

"Well, Lauren Adams, you have made one old man very happy." He paused and glanced at Jesse. "Come to think of it, it looks as if you've made one young man very happy also, but that's another matter."

Jesse saved her from a response. "Lauren, this is Luke Ebsin."

"Enough niceties, Jesse." Luke handed Jesse the map. "I have something to show you."

Jesse uncoiled the map. "I don't understand."

"What's not to understand? It's Coosa."

A low moan escaped Jesse as he traced the squiggly lines that crisscrossed a map of the state. "What—five miles to the west of the original excavation site?"

"Exactly." Luke tapped a thin yellow line. "Using our old theories and the new coordinates based on Lauren's find, Coosa is exactly where we said it was."

Jesse raised his eyebrows.

Luke cleared his throat, a sly grin emerging on his face. "Well, not exactly, but I'm still looking forward to saying 'I told you so.' " He cuffed Jesse on the arm. "Which is just what I'm about to do."

He waved his thin arms in the air. "Gather around, everyone. We're about to have a staff meeting."

Luke spread the map on the hood of Ken's dusty car. As the members of the commission began walking toward them, Luke turned to Jesse. "You're dismissed. After all, you're the only one that I don't have to prove this to." His gaze softened. "You're the only one who ever believed in me."

The two men seemed lost in a private thought for a long moment before Jesse spoke. "You taught me everything I know."

Luke winked at Lauren. "Then run like hell, son. The stuffed shirts are on their way."

Jesse laughed and clasped Lauren around the shoulders. He raised his voice for the others to hear. "I'm just going to help Miss Adams with her things."

Lauren nestled closer to him as they walked away. "What things?" she asked.

He shrugged. "Beats me. But I'm not through talking to you just yet."

As they reached the house, she climbed the porch stairs in front of him. "Yes, sir, Sergeant McCain," she said. She saluted as Jesse walked through the door.

"That's Professor McCain to you, Private," he said, drawing her into his arms.

"What?" she tilted her head back to look at him.

He smiled. "The university has offered me a teaching position."

"Jesse, that's wonderful," she said, hugging him.

"But is that what you want? I never really pictured you staying in one place."

His smile turned to a scowl. "Just what did you picture?" he asked.

She thought a minute. "Let's see . . . How about you and Ken taking an exciting position on some tropical excavation, swarming with beautiful women and drinking wine until dawn?"

"Well . . . Replace the women with mosquitoes and you're pretty much on target." He pulled her against him, lifting her until her hips were cradled against his. "But that was the past," he whispered into her ear as he slowly lowered her back down to the floor.

Lauren felt her muscles go limp as the warm rush of his breath caressed her neck. The sound of muted voices penetrated their quiet world, though, and she was reminded of the men who waited outside. She pulled back, seeing several new smudges of dirt dotting Jesse's shirt. She ran her thumb over one, thinking that the men would know what they'd been up to.

"I guess they're waiting on you, huh?" She sighed. "But can you tell me what's going on first?"

Jesse threw back his head and laughed. "There you go again, asking two questions at once."

She grinned. "You made love to me, then left without a word. Taking, I might add, some very valuable artifacts with you. You came back, kissed me in front of a bunch of strangers, talked in some alien archaeologist gibberish, and now—" She put her hands on her hips. "I think I deserve an explanation."

"You're right." He pushed his hands into her hair, and pulled her to him, tenderly kissing her forehead. "But how could you have possibly thought I'd leave you without a word, much less take off with the coin and the arrowheads?"

She rubbed her hands over his wrists, loving the feel of his strength beneath her fingers. "I thought maybe you were tempted."

"The only thing that tempts me is you," he said, kissing her neck. "Besides, if I'd sold every artifact I took, it would probably only get me airfare to say, Tupelo, Mississippi."

"You're serious?" she asked. "If the coin isn't worth much, then what's the big stir? I doubt those men out there are waiting to see me finish draining the pond."

He stepped back to look at her and cocked an eyebrow. "I don't know . . ."

Lauren hit him.

"The coin is extremely valuable," he said. "Priceless, in fact. But only in the context of where it was found. Have you ever heard of the Spanish explorer Tristan de Luna?"

Lauren hooked her thumb over her shoulder, indicating the stack of library books visible in the kitchen. "I haven't spent so much time with him since grade school."

"Well, then you know he came to America to retrace the steps of the famous explorer Hernando de Soto."

"A helluva guy," Lauren added.

Jesse laughed. "Yeah, he was a real sweetheart. Pillaging and plundering were his strong suit. Anyway, the routes Soto and Luna took through Alabama have never been proven."

Lauren nodded. "I've read a little about it."

"Believe me, it's a big deal to us groundhogs." Jesse smiled. "And the coin, along with the container, prove beyond a doubt that the Tristan de Luna expedition occupied this land. The Early Exploration Commission has been searching for proof like this since the nineteen thirties."

Lauren was overwhelmed by the thought. "And now you know where the Coosa chiefdom is as well."

He smiled. "It looks that way. Thanks to you, we have new coordinates to base our old theories on."

"But wait a minute. What container are you talking about?"

Jesse's dimple showed again. "Remember the brass container the arrowheads were stored in?"

She nodded.

"It's Spanish. Sixteenth century. Its location was labeled. . . ." He paused, looking a little sheepish. "As found near the willow tree at the creek. The same place you found the coin. My guess is that it's a burial mound."

She grinned and spread her arms wide. "You owe me a huge apology."

"Well, I'm going to be around to give you one," he said, looking intently into her eyes. "If that's okay with you."

"I don't understand." She had assumed the conversation she'd overheard between Jesse and Ken had meant that he was giving up his apartment to leave town. Her heart skipped a beat. "You won't be teaching at the university in Tuscaloosa?"

"I will," he said. "But after we've completed the excavation." He winked at her. "They've asked me to oversee the Adams/McCain site. The complete excavation will take years. Can you put up with me for that long?"

She reached around him to tug his ponytail. "And longer."

"There's one more thing."

"What's that?"

He slowly traced his index finger down her jawline until it came to rest on her mouth. Leaning down, he kissed her. "I want to do that over and over again for the rest of my life," he said.

Tears stung the backs of her eyes. "So what's stopping you?" she asked.

"Absolutely nothing if you'll say yes. But I mean the whole nine yards. For better or for worse." His expression was deadly serious. "Is the answer still yes?"

She nodded.

He pulled her into his arms, hugging her as if he would never stop. And she didn't want him to.

"I missed you so much," he whispered into the crook of her neck. "I thought I could smell your perfume when I got back to my apartment the other night."

Lauren bit her lip, considering a confession. No, that was one secret she'd keep for now. "You have an active imagination, Jesse McCain." Standing on tiptoe, she whispered into his ear, "Let's put it to use."

He grinned down at her. "What about the commission?"

She smiled. "If they've been waiting for sixty-some-odd years, they can wait a little longer."

"You know something?" Jesse said. "You're absolutely right."

THE EDITORS' CORNER

February is on the way, which can mean only one thing—it's time for Treasured Tales V! In our continuing tradition, LOVESWEPT presents four spectacular new romances inspired by age-old myths, fairy tales, and legends.

LOVESWEPT favorite Laura Taylor weaves a tapestry of love across the threads of time in **CLOUD DANCER**, LOVESWEPT #822. Smoke, flames, and a cry for help call Clayton Sloan to the rescue, but the fierce Cheyenne warrior is shocked to find himself a hero in an unknown time. Torn by fate from all that he loves, Clay is anchored only by his longing for Kelly Farrell, the brave woman who knows his secret and the torment that shadows his nights. In this breathtaking journey through history, Laura Taylor once more demonstrates her unique storytelling gifts in a moving evocation of the healing power of love.

A chance encounter turns into a passionate journey for two in **DESTINY UNKNOWN**, LOVESWEPT #823, from the talented Maris Soule. He grins at the cool beauty whose grip on a fluffy dog is about to slip, but Cody Taylor gets even more pleasure from noticing Bernadette Sanders's reaction to his down and dirty appearance. Common sense tells the sleek store executive not to get sidetracked by the glint in the maverick builder's eyes. But when he seeks her out time and time again, daring to challenge her expectations, to ignite her desire, she succumbs to her hunger for the unconventional rogue. Maris Soule demonstrates why romantic chemistry can be so deliciously explosive.

From award-winning author Suzanne Brockmann comes **OTHERWISE ENGAGED**, LOVESWEPT #824. Funny, charismatic, and one heck of a temptation, Preston Seaholm makes a wickedly sexy hero as he rescues Molly Cassidy from tumbling off the roof! The pretty widow bewitches him with a smile, unaware that the tanned sun god is Sunrise Key's mysterious tycoon—and one of the most eligible bachelors in the country. He needs her help to fend off unwanted advances, but once he's persuaded her to play along at pretending they're engaged, he finds himself helplessly surrendering to her temptation. As fast-paced and touching as it is sensual, this is another winner from Suzanne Brockmann.

Last but not least, Kathy Lynn Emerson offers a hero who learns to **LOVE THY NEIGHBOR**, LOVESWEPT #825. The moment she drives up in a flame-red Mustang to claim the crumbling house next door, Marshall Austin knows he was right. Linnea Bryan is bewitching, a fascinating puzzle who can easily hold him spellbound—but she is also the daughter of the woman who destroyed his parents' marriage. So he launches his campaign to send her packing. But even as he insists he wants her out of town by nightfall, his heart is really saying he wants her all night long. Kathy Lynn Emerson draws the battle lines, then lets the seduction begin in her LOVESWEPT debut!

Happy reading!

With warmest wishes,

Beth de Guzman

Shauna Summers

Beth de Guzman   Shauna Summers
Senior Editor   Editor

P.S. Watch for these Bantam women's fiction titles coming in February: Available for the first time in paperback is the *New York Times* bestseller **GUILTY AS SIN** by the new master of suspense, Tami Hoag. Jane Feather, author of the nationally bestselling *VICE* and *VALENTINE*, is set to thrill romance lovers once again with **THE DIAMOND SLIPPER**, a tale of passion and intrigue involving a forced bride, a reluctant hero, and a jeweled charm. And finally, from Michelle Martin comes **STOLEN HEARTS**, a contemporary romance in the tradition of Jayne Ann Krentz in which an ex–jewel thief pulls the con of her life, but one man is determined to catch her—and never let her get away. Don't miss the previews of these exceptional novels in next month's LOVE-SWEPTs. And immediately following this page, sneak a peek at the Bantam women's fiction titles on sale *now*!

For current information on Bantam's women's fiction, visit our new web site, *Isn't It Romantic,* at the following address: **http://www.bdd.com/romance**

Don't miss these terrific novels
by your favorite Bantam authors

On sale in December:

HAWK O'TOOLE'S HOSTAGE
by Sandra Brown

THE UGLY DUCKLING
by Iris Johansen

WICKED
by Susan Johnson

HEART OF THE FALCON
by Suzanne Robinson

Sandra Brown

Her heady blend of passion, humor, and high-voltage romantic suspense has made her one of the most beloved writers in America. Now the author of more than two dozen New York Times bestsellers weaves a thrilling tale of a woman who finds herself at the mercy of a handsome stranger—and the treacherous feelings only he can arouse. . . .

HAWK O'TOOLE'S HOSTAGE

A classic Bantam romance available in hardcover for the first time in December 1996

To Hawk O'Toole, she was a pawn in a desperate gamble to help his people. To Miranda Price, he was a stranger who'd done the unthinkable: kidnapped her and her young son from a train full of sight-seeing vacationers. Now held hostage on a distant reservation for reasons she cannot at first fathom, Miranda finds herself battling a captor who is by turns harsh and tender, mysteriously aloof, and dangerously seductive.

Hawk assumed that Miranda, the beautiful ex-wife of Representative Price, would be as selfish and immoral as the tabloids suggested. Instead, she seems genuinely afraid for her son's life—and willing to risk her own to keep his safe. But, committed to a fight he didn't start, Hawk knows he can't afford to feel anything but contempt for his prisoner. To force the government to reopen the Lone Puma Mine, he must keep Miranda at arm's length, to remember that she is his enemy—even when she ignites his deepest desires.

Slowly, Miranda begins to learn what drives this brooding, solitary man, to discover the truth about his tragic past. But it will take a shocking revelation to finally force her to face her own past and the woman she's become . . . and to ask herself: Is it freedom she really wants . . . or the chance to stay with Hawk forever?

"Only Iris Johansen can so magically mix a love story with hair-raising adventure and suspense. Don't miss this page-turner."—Catherine Coulter

THE UGLY DUCKLING

by *New York Times* bestselling author

Iris Johansen

now available in paperback

Plain, soft-spoken Nell Calder isn't the type of woman to inspire envy, lust—or murderous passion. Until one night when the unimaginable happens, and her life, her dreams, her future, are shattered by a brutal attack. Though badly hurt, she emerges from the nightmare a woman transformed, with an exquisitely beautiful face and strong, lithe body. While Nicholas Tanek, a mysterious stranger who compels both fear and fascination, gives her a reason to go on living. But divulging the identity of her assailant to Nell might just turn out to be the biggest mistake of Tanek's life. For he will soon find his carefully laid plans jeopardized by Nell's daring to strike out on her own.

He had come for nothing, Nicholas thought in disgust as he gazed down at the surf crashing on the rocks below. No one would want to kill Nell Calder. She was no more likely to be connected with Gardeaux than that big-eyed elf she was now lavishing with French pastry and adoration.

If there was a target here, it was probably Kavinski. As head of an emerging Russian state, he had the power to be either a cash cow or extremely troublesome to Gardeaux. Nell Calder wouldn't be considered troublesome to anyone. He had known the answers to all the questions he had asked her, but he had wanted to see her reactions. He had been watching her all evening, and it was clear she was a nice, shy woman, totally out of her depth even with those fairly innocuous sharks downstairs. He couldn't imagine her having enough influence to warrant bribery, and she would never have been able to deal one-on-one with Gardeaux.

Unless she was more than she appeared. Possibly. She seemed as meek as a lamb, but she'd had the guts to toss him out of her daughter's room.

Everyone fought back if the battle was important enough. And it was important for Nell Calder not to share her daughter with him. No, the list must mean something else. When he went back downstairs, he would stay close to Kavinski.

> *"Here we go up, up, up*
> *High in the sky so blue.*
> *Here we go down, down, down*
> *Touching the rose so red."*

She was singing to the kid. He had always liked lullabies. There was a reassuring continuity about them that had been missing in his own life. Since the dawn of time, mothers had sung to their children, and they would probably still be singing to them a thousand years from then.

The song ended with a low chuckle and a murmur he couldn't hear.

She came out of the bedroom and closed the door

a few minutes later. She was flushed and glowing with an expression as soft as melted butter.

"I've never heard that lullaby before," he said.

She looked startled, as if she'd forgotten he was still there. "It's very old. My grandmother used to sing it to me."

"Is your daughter asleep?"

"No, but she will be soon. I started the music box for her again. By the time it finishes, she usually nods off."

"She's a beautiful child."

"Yes." A luminous smile turned her plain face radiant once more. "Yes, she is."

He stared at her, intrigued. He found he wanted to keep that smile on her face. "And bright?"

"Sometimes too bright. Her imagination can be troublesome. But she's always reasonable and you can talk to—" She broke off and her eagerness faded. "But this can't interest you. I forgot the tray. I'll go back for it."

"Don't bother. You'll disturb Jill. The maid can pick it up in the morning."

She gave him a level glance. "That's what I told you."

He smiled. "But then I didn't want to listen. Now it makes perfect sense to me."

"Because it's what you want to do."

"Exactly."

"I have to go back too. I haven't met Kavinski yet." She moved toward the door.

"Wait. I think you'll want to remove that chocolate from your gown first."

"Damn." She frowned as she looked down at the stain on the skirt. "I forgot." She turned toward the bathroom and said dryly, "Go on. I assure you I don't need your help with this problem."

He hesitated.

She glanced at him pointedly over her shoulder.

He had no excuse for staying, not that that small fact would have deterred him.

But he also had no reason. He had lived by his wits too long not to trust his instincts, and this woman wasn't a target of any sort. He should be watching Kavinski.

He turned toward the door. "I'll tell the maid you're ready for her to come back."

"Thank you, that's very kind of you," she said automatically as she disappeared into the bathroom.

Good manners obviously instilled from childhood. Loyalty. Gentleness. A nice woman whose world was centered on that sweet kid. He had definitely drawn a blank.

The maid wasn't waiting in the hallway. He'd have to send up one of the servants from downstairs.

He moved quickly through the corridors and started down the staircase.

Shots.

Coming from the ballroom.

Christ.

He tore down the stairs.

WICKED

by Susan Johnson

"An exceptional writer."—*Affaire de Coeur*

Serena Blythe's plans to escape a life of servitude had gone terribly awry. So she took the only course left to her. She sneaked aboard a sleek yacht about to set sail—and found herself face-to-face with a dangerous sensual stranger. Beau St. Jules, the Earl of Rochefort, had long surpassed his father's notoriety as a libertine. Less well known was his role as intelligence-gatherer for England. Yet even on a mission to seek vital war information, he couldn't resist practicing his well-polished seduction on the beautiful, disarmingly innocent stowaway. And in the weeks to come, with battles breaking out on the Continent and Serena's life in peril, St. Jules would risk everything to rescue the one woman who'd finally captured his heart.

"Your life sounds idyllic. Unlike mine of late," Serena said with a fleeting grimace. "But I intend to change that."

Frantic warning bells went off in Beau's consciousness. Had she *deliberately* come on board? Were her designing relatives even now in hot pursuit? Or were they explaining the ruinous details to his father instead? "How exactly," he softly inquired, his dark eyes wary, "do you plan on facilitating those changes?"

"Don't be alarmed," she said, suddenly grinning. "I have no designs on you."

He laughed, his good spirits instantly restored. "Candid women have always appealed to me."

"While men with yachts are out of my league." Her smile was dazzling. "But why don't you deal us another hand," she cheerfully said, "and I'll see what I can do about mending my fortunes."

She was either completely ingenuous or the most skillful coquette. But he had more than enough money to indulge her, and she amused him immensely.

He dealt the cards.

And when the beefsteaks arrived sometime later, the cards were put away and they both tucked into the succulent meat with gusto.

She ate with a quiet intensity, absorbed in the food and the act of eating. It made him consider his casual acceptance of all the privileges in his life with a new regard. But only briefly, because he was very young, very wealthy, too handsome for complete humility, and beset by intense carnal impulses that were profoundly immune to principle.

He'd simply offer her a liberal settlement when the *Siren* docked in Naples, he thought, discarding any further moral scruples.

He glanced at the clock.

Three-thirty.

They'd be making love in the golden light of dawn . . . or sooner perhaps, he thought with a faint smile, reaching across the small table to refill her wineglass.

"This must be heaven or very near . . ." Serena murmured, looking up from cutting another portion of beefsteak. "I can't thank you enough."

"Remy deserves all the credit."

"You're very disarming. And kind."

"You're very beautiful, Miss Blythe. And a damned good card player."

"Papa practiced with me. He was an accomplished player when he wasn't drinking."

"Have you thought of making your fortune in the gaming rooms instead of wasting your time as an underpaid governess?"

"No," she softly said, her gaze direct.

"Forgive me. I meant no rudeness. But the demimonde is not without its charm."

"I'm sure it is for a man," she said, taking a squarely cut piece of steak off her fork with perfect white teeth. "However, I'm going to art school in Florence," she went on, beginning to chew. "And I shall make my living painting."

"Painting what?"

She chewed a moment more, savoring the flavors, then swallowed. "Portraits, of course. Where the money is. I shall be flattering in the extreme. I'm very good, you know."

"I'm sure you are." And he intended to find out how good she was in other ways as well. "Why don't I give you your first commission?" He'd stopped eating but he'd not stopped drinking, and he gazed at her over the rim of his wineglass.

"I don't have my paints. They're on the *Betty Lee* with my luggage."

"We could put ashore in Portugal and buy you some. How much do you charge?"

Her gaze shifted from her plate. "Nothing for you. You've been generous in the extreme. I'd be honored to paint you"—she paused and smiled—"whoever you are."

"Beau St. Jules."

"*The* Beau St. Jules?" She put her flatware down and openly studied him. "The darling of the broadsheets . . . London's premier rake who's outsinned his father, The Saint?" A note of teasing had entered her voice, a familiar, intimate reflection occasioned by the numerous glasses of wine she'd drunk. "Should I be alarmed?"

He shook his head, amusement in his eyes. "I'm very ordinary," he modestly said, this man who stood stud to all the London beauties. "You needn't be alarmed."

He wasn't ordinary, of course, not in any way. He was the gold standard, she didn't doubt, by which male beauty was judged. His perfect features and artfully cropped black hair reminded her of classic Greek sculpture; his overt masculinity, however, was much less the refined cultural ideal. He was startlingly male.

"Aren't rakes older? You're very young," she declared. And gorgeous as a young god, she decided, although the cachet of his notorious reputation probably wasn't based on his beauty alone. He was very charming.

He shrugged at her comment on his age. He'd begun his carnal amusements very young he could have said, but, circumspect, asked instead, "How old are *you?*" His smile was warm, personal. "Out in the world on your own?"

"Twenty-three." Her voice held a small defiance; a single lady of three and twenty was deemed a spinster in any society.

"A very nice age," he pleasantly noted, his dark eyes lazily half-lidded. "Do you like floating islands?"

She looked at him blankly.

"The dessert."

"Oh, yes, of course." She smiled. "I should save room then."

By all means, he licentiously thought, nodding a smiling approval, filling their wineglasses once more. *Save room for me—because I'm coming in. . . .*

Blazing with romance, intrigue, and the splendor of ancient Egypt

HEART OF THE FALCON

The bestselling

Suzanne Robinson

at her finest

All her life, raven-haired Anqet had basked in the tranquillity of Nefer . . . until the day her father died and her uncle descended upon the estate, hungry for her land, hungry for her. Desperate to escape his cruel obsession, she fled. But now, masquerading as a commoner in the magnificent city of Thebes, Anqet faces a new danger. Mysterious and seductive, Count Seth seems to be a loyal soldier to the pharaoh. Yet soon Anqet will find that he's drawn her back into a web of treachery and desire, where one false move could end her life and his fiery passion could brand her soul.

Anqet waited for the procession to pass. She had asked for directions to the Street of the Scarab. If she was correct, this alley would lead directly to her goal. She followed the dusty, shaded path between windowless buildings, eager to reach the house of Lady Gasantra before dark. She hadn't eaten since leaving her barber companion and his family earlier in the afternoon, and her stomach rumbled noisily. She hoped Tamit would remember her. They hadn't seen each other for several years.

The alley twisted back and forth several times, but Anqet at last saw the intersection with the Street of the Scarab. Intent upon reaching the end of her journey, she ran into the road, into the path of an oncoming chariot.

There was a shout, then the screams of outraged horses as the driver of the chariot hauled his animals back. Anqet ducked to the ground beneath pawing hooves. Swerving, the vehicle skidded and tipped. The horses reared and stamped, showering stones and dust over Anqet.

From behind the bronze-plated chariot came a stream of oaths. Someone pounced on Anqet from the vehicle, hauling her to her feet by her hair, and shaking her roughly.

"You little gutter-frog! I ought to whip you for dashing about like a demented antelope. You could have caused one of my horses to break a leg."

Anqet's head rattled on her shoulders. Surprised, she bore with this treatment for a few moments before stamping on a sandaled foot. There was a yelp. The shaking stopped, but now two strong hands gripped her wrists. Silence reigned while her attacker recovered from his pain, then a new string of obscenities rained upon her. The retort she thought up never passed her lips, for when she raised her eyes to those of the charioteer, she forgot her words.

Eyes of deep green, the color of the leaves of a water lily. Eyes weren't supposed to be green. Eyes were brown, or black, and they didn't glaze with the molten fury of the Lake of Fire in the *Book of the Dead*. Anqet stared into those pools of malachite until, at a call behind her, they shifted to look over her head.

"Count Seth! My lord, are you injured?"

"No, Dega. See to the horses while I deal with this, this . . ."

Anqet stared up at the count while he spoke to his servant. He was unlike any man she had ever seen. Tall, slender, with lean, catlike muscles, he had wide shoulders that were in perfect proportion to his flat torso and long legs. He wore a short soldier's kilt belted around his hips. A bronze corselet stretched tight across his wide chest; leather bands protected his wrists and accentuated elegant, long-fingered hands that gripped Anqet in a numbing hold. Anqet gazed back at Count Seth and noted the strange auburn tint of the silky hair that fell almost to his shoulders. He was beautiful. Exotic and beautiful, and wildly furious.

Count Seth snarled at her. "You're fortunate my team wasn't hurt, or I'd take their cost out on your hide."

Anqet's temper flared. She forgot that she was supposed to be a humble commoner. Her chin came up, her voice raised in command.

"Release me at once."

Shock made Count Seth obey the order. No woman spoke to him thus. For the first time, he really looked at the girl before him. She faced him squarely and met his gaze, not with the humility or appreciation he was used to, but with the anger of an equal.

Bareka! What an uncommonly beautiful commoner. Where in the Two Lands had she gotten those fragile features? Her face was enchanting. High-arched brows curved over enormous black eyes that glittered with highlights of brown and inspected him as if he were a stray dog.

Seth let his eyes rest for a moment on her lips. To watch them move made him want to lick them. He appraised the fullness of her breasts and the length of her legs. To his chagrin, he felt a wave of desire pulse through his veins and settle demandingly in his groin.

Curse the girl. She had stirred him past control. Well, he was never one to neglect an opportunity. What else could be expected of a barbarian half-breed?

Seth moved with the swiftness of an attacking lion, pulling the girl to him. She fit perfectly against his body. Her soft flesh made him want to thrust his hips against her, right in the middle of the street. He cursed as she squirmed against him in a futile effort to escape and further tortured his barely leashed senses.

"Release me!"

Seth uttered a light, mocking laugh. "Compose yourself, my sweet. Surely you won't mind repaying me for my inconvenience?"

DON'T MISS THESE FABULOUS
BANTAM WOMEN'S FICTION TITLES

On Sale in January

GUILTY AS SIN
by TAMI HOAG

The terror that began in *Night Sins* continues in this spine-chilling *New York Times* bestseller. Now available in paperback.

_____ 56452-8 $6.50/$8.99

THE DIAMOND SLIPPER
by the incomparable JANE FEATHER
nationally bestselling author of Vice *and* Vanity

With her delightful wit and gift for storytelling, Jane Feather brings to life the breathtaking tale of a determined heroine, a sinister lover, and the intrigue of a mysterious past in this, the first book of her new Charm Bracelet trilogy.

_____ 57523-6 $5.99/$7.99

From the fresh new voice of MICHELLE MARTIN
STOLEN HEARTS

This sparkling romance in the tradition of Jayne Ann Krentz tells the tale of an ex-jewel thief who pulls the con of her life and the one man who is determined to catch her—and never let her get away.

_____ 57648-8 $5.50/$7.50